The Wages of Sin

For six years, the *Free Aristotle Macho Edwards* campaign has pulled a variety of exotic publicity stunts. To ITN crime reporter Kate Lewis, FAME is hot news; but to her fiancé, Chief Inspector Taff Roberts, it's a racket. To him, Ari Edwards is a black pimp who fully deserves his life-sentence for the brutal murder of one of his high-society prostitutes.

But then a crucial new witness disappears and the detectives on the original case start pressuring Taff to get at Kate—who is then grossly assaulted.

Retaliating, Taff eventually gets the murder conviction quashed and Ari Edwards released . . . but to fatal consequences as those behind the pimp's conviction—senior police and a top City company—close ranks to conceal their involvement.

by the same author

GAMELORD
AN ABUSE OF JUSTICE
RIOT

———————

THE FOURTH MONKEY

ROGER PARKES

The Wages of Sin

THE CRIME CLUB
An Imprint of HarperCollins *Publishers*

First published in Great Britain in 1992
by The Crime Club, an imprint of
HarperCollins Publishers, 77–85 Fulham Palace Road,
Hammersmith, London W6 8JB

9 8 7 6 5 4 3 2 1

Roger Parkes asserts the moral right to be identified
as the author of this work.

A catalogue record for this book is
available from the British Library

ISBN 0 00 232394 X

Photoset in Linotron Baskerville by
Rowland Phototypesetting Ltd
Bury St Edmunds, Suffolk
Printed and bound in Great Britain by
HarperCollins Book Manufacturing, Glasgow

To lovely Tessa

CHAPTER 1

Two demonstrators were arrested this morning after climbing the giant Norwegian Christmas tree in Trafalgar Square. Later, public works officials used a crane to remove a large banner which had been hoisted up the tree. Reading Free Aristotle Macho Edwards, *the banner was apparently the latest bid in the six-year campaign by Mrs Bella Edwards to win a review of her husband's conviction for the murder of prostitute Arlene Milton. Later this morning at Horseferry Road Magistrates' Court the two demonstrators are expected to face charges of damaging the tree.*

And no doubt, mused Chief Inspector Taff Roberts, listening to the news report on his way to the office, Bella will stage a mini-Caribbean carnival outside the court for the benefit of the TV cameras. Rather too chilly for the limbo girls to dance topless this time perhaps, but for sure she'd have dreamed up a good visual to boost the TV spectacle of a darn great FAME banner draped over the Trafalgar Square tree.

Taff, as behoves a man in love, found himself laughing. No matter that he was having to slow up for a motorway tailback, he simply found FAME's endless gimmicks funny.

Not that he approved of their aims. As far as the policeman side of him was concerned, they were just a bunch of minority-group opportunists cashing in on the conviction of a black pimp for a particularly brutal killing. Although Taff had not been involved with the investigation of the murder, there'd been no shortage of lurid press reports on the trial—reports enlivened with recurring courtroom protests over pro-Crown rulings by His Honour Judge Willis. But from the reports, Taff reckoned the case against Edwards sounded solid enough, if largely circumstantial.

However, the FAME campaign itself, thanks to the unflagging energy and ingenuity of the campaigners, not least of Bella Edwards herself, was an essential study for all students of media manipulation, Taff Roberts included. Paradoxically, the campaign was notable also for the persistence of its failure: Ari Edwards remained not one breath nearer to freedom.

With the tailback now totally stationary, the copper telephoned headquarters to find out why, then pulled out of the stalled traffic and, headlights on, drove forward along the hard shoulder. A mile or so ahead he saw a police helicopter lift off and zoom away from the scene of the accident. Then, hearing an ambulance coming at full belt behind him, he eased on to the verge to let it pass before following in its wake.

There were a couple of crews of motorway police there already, those out near the overturned lorry all wearing gas-masks, as were the firemen. A couple of constables were working along advising drivers as a precaution to vacate their vehicles. Taff was directed to a uniformed inspector, his face flushed with anxiety, his eyes red and streaming as if from grief.

'CI Roberts, public relations.' Taff held out his warrant card. 'I imagine you haven't contacted the press office yet.'

'Jesus in Heaven!'

'Sorry, Inspector, but these days the public hear about things almost before they happen.' He reached for a notepad. 'Just how toxic is the spillage from those drums?'

It turned out the driver was either too injured or too foreign to give intelligible answers; and as yet no one had been able to contact the German suppliers or find a German-speaker to interpret the information printed on the drums. Whatever the viscous brew seeping across the tarmac, a breeze was wafting its fumes lazily along the eastern line of stalled traffic. The spilt liquid smelt of violets, suggesting a harmless domestic product. But if so, why was it stinging their eyes and the back of their throats? And how reactive might it get when slurping over the motorway?

'The chopper's supposed to be bringing us some sort of

boffin.' The Inspector snorted in irony. 'Likely they'll send us some chemical-warfare freak from Aldermaston.'

'So?' Taff grinned. 'This stuff's from Germany, *ja*.'

The inspector snorted again, glad to resort to flippancy. 'And violet-scented, *mein Herr*. Fiendishly cunning.'

Taff nodded towards his car. 'Right, I'll get on to my office to ring round a press release.' Then, seeing the anguish flushing the inspector's face, he added: 'I know, mate, I know, but this is the age of the car phone. Act pronto and we just might prevent Radio 210 plunging the entire Thames Valley into panic.'

Heading back to his car, Taff wondered whether the officer's attitude—the hint of coldness and suspicion towards him—was personal. Of course it was reasonable for an inspector in charge of a critical-accident situation to resent interference by a fellow officer—especially one linked to the bloody press. None the less, since Taff's return from secondment to Scotland Yard, he'd been picking up hostile vibes too often from his Thames Valley colleagues; and the clear message was that CI Roberts was no longer regarded as one of the lads so much as a C-Ten nark, more adept at spying on his brother officers than supporting them.

Taff Roberts's most recent stint with the Met, investigating the collapse of numerous football-hooligan prosecutions, had been mentioned only briefly by his boss, Superintendent Lynn Jordan, during the first limb of his annual interview the previous day. In fact that first part of the interview had been little more than a formality, the Super merely asking a few routine questions before ticking the relevant boxes on the blue form, then filling in the lower section as a preliminary to the far more probing second phase of the interview, due the next day with their chief superintendent.

No problems then, David? Lynn had asked. *Settling in all right?* Taff's confirmation had been genuine enough: he enjoyed the variety of cases PR brought him to and, thanks to his fiancée, Kate, he reckoned he could cope with reporters. His real problem ran far deeper, relating to his overall career as a copper: whether to stay on for senior rank or whether to pack it all in, go back to college and read law. It was an issue which might not have existed but for his recurring troubles with the Metropolitan force. Certainly, those troubles were the reason officers like the one at the motorway spill sometimes eyed him askance. It was an attitude which, in a force still largely reliant on macho chauvinism and hard-drinking bonhomie, was tough to live with. No matter that Taff's conscience was clear, the stigma was unlikely to fade for a long while yet.

Not finding the commuting from London too heavy? Too bloody right he was! Yet he had shrugged off Lynn's question, anxious not to be drawn on his domestic situation. However, his reticence was less to do with the fact that his choice of partner was ITN's chief crime reporter, so much as the question of why he and Kate hadn't found a home nearer to TVP headquarters at Kidlington. It was a touchy issue all round: his bosses expected it, if only as a gesture of commitment; Taff longed to escape the Smoke as much as the Met; but Kate felt her job depended on her availability. Although she was probably mistaken, her certainty stemmed from her chronic sense of insecurity, about which Taff could do naught.

Not finding the press hounds too yappy? Of course, being engaged to one does greatly help. Indeed, the decision to assign CI Roberts to PR appeared to be a tacit acceptance by the Thames Valley brass of his live-in relationship with the notorious Kate Lewis: since CI Roberts seemed downright incapable of living without the blessed woman, best make a virtue of necessity and assign him to media liaison. Yet this was a mixed blessing for the happy couple, Taff having to be extra careful not to favour Kate with anything other than official-release stuff.

'Any problems over the spillage story, Tony?'

Taff knew without having to listen that Sergeant Warboys's answer would be one of polite reassurance. Even had he received a full-scale blast from the Press Council, Tony

Warboys would contrive to dismiss it so as to preserve his precious image of capability.

'The only problem, sir, could be for you.' The sergeant held out a piece of paper with a name and number on it. 'Specifically a Commander Hammond, calling you twenty minutes ago from the Yard on extension 8154.'

'Why should that be a problem?'

Warboys shrugged. 'Solely his tone of voice, sir. Reply at your earliest, and all that.'

Taff went into his office and shut the door, reluctant to ring the commander without knowing a little more. He had never met Hammond personally, knew him solely by reputation as a career climber who had landed one or two prominent investigations when he was a CID superintendent. A check with the Yard's switchboard revealed that extension 8154 belonged to the prosecutions section. None the wiser, Taff asked to be connected.

'Yes, Roberts, I just wanted a brief and, let me stress, totally informal word.' Warboys was right about the frosty tone of voice.

'As you wish, Commander.'

'What I wish is that I hadn't been obliged to contact you at all.' He cleared his throat, and Taff braced himself for yet another re-emergence of the Met spectre: would the damned thing never cease to haunt him? In the event, it turned out to be the other spectre in his life.

'It concerns your, er, relationship with Miss Lewis. Nothing irregular, of course: officers are entitled to private lives, so long as they're discreet. However, given the slightest hint of indiscretion, things start to get a bit blurred. Savvy?'

'Not really, no.' Taff could get as touchy about Kate as he could about being a Welshman.

'You'll appreciate, of course, that I'm talking about the Aristotle Edwards case.' It clicked instantly in Taff's mind how it was Hammond who, as a DCS, had taken the credit for the Edwards conviction; he could recall the man's bland self-satisfaction as he faced the cameras soon after the verdict. But what a pain the strident protests of Bella and her

FAME team must have been to him ever since. He had
landed a sensational murder conviction, won acclaim all
round and promotion along with it. But then up had
popped Bella and her team with their endless press gimmicks, proclaiming racial prejudice and injustice, police
corruption, an Establishment cover-up, di-dah-di-dah-di-
dah, as multiple grounds for a retrial. Emphatically not
favourite with Commander Hammond.

'I don't see what the Edwards case has to do with me.'

'Come off it, Roberts. It's frankly nauseating the air space
ITN give the wretched woman. Totally predictable, of
course, given the smut angle—pimps and toms and Cabinet
bimbos and all. But as for offering us any sort of right of
reply—oh dear no!'

'Commander, I can understand your angst over it all.
But as to where I fit in—'

'Damn it, your—your lady is ITN. More, she seems to
act as the bitch's personal minder!'

Taff forced himself to pause before replying. 'Look, even
if I'd ever discussed the FAME story with my fiancée, there
is no way I could possibly influence her handling of it. I'm
prepared to pass on your request for a right of reply, if
you're sure that would be a prudent move. But—'

'Roberts, we all know about your personal crusade
against the Met.' Then, topping Taff's indignant denial:
'All right then, should you wish to build some bridges, show
some good will, here's an opportunity.'

'Even if I did, I'm not my fiancée's keeper.'

'Ah. Well, no, seeing her on TV, I can believe that.
However, as a press officer, you're fully aware of the con-
straints regarding leaks of sensitive information.'

'Now look—'

'Abuses of which can provoke severe disciplinary action.'
Then, once again over-riding Taff's reply: 'Most especially,
leaks from CRO or case files.'

'If you're accusing me—'

'Of course not, Roberts.' The tone was suddenly more
conciliatory. First show the iron fist, then pull on the velvet

glove. 'Simply passing on a word of caution. The Edwards case has provoked a lot of angst, as you rightly observed.'

'Anything else—sir?'

'Simply to ask you, as one officer to another, to do anything you can to get your lady—your fiancée—to lay off.'

'I already told you—'

'At the very least, to encourage her to report the story in a more balanced and responsible way. Understood?' Pause. 'My very best regards to Chief Superintendent Marsh when you next see him.'

There was no sign of the chemical spill by the time Taff headed home along the M40 that evening: the crashed German truck and its freight all removed, the household cleaning fluid all cleaned away, nothing to mark the spot but an unnaturally scrubbed stretch of motorway and the lingering fragrance of violets.

But, *diawl*, to hell with a job where one's superiors could resort to shabby threats and intimidation like that! Totally out of the blue, the bastard inferring CRO leaks and so on which were totally without foundation! On the contrary, Taff made it a rule to tell Kate absolutely nothing that wasn't destined for a formal press release. More, that was how Kate wanted it, insisting their affair was strictly personal and nothing to do with any leaks or privileges. Or so she said.

So why stay on in the damn job? Why go on getting aggro from prats like Hammond, enduring the enmity of the Met and, worse, sensing the distrust of his Thames Valley colleagues? The law was wide open to him as a career. Not as one of those fat-cat, fee-grubbing, corporate lawyers, but the more decent if threadbare breed to be found on the Legal Aid duty rosters. Kate was all for it, if only to put an end to pressures from the likes of Hammond. Or so she said.

'It might have helped a bit if I'd known about Bella Edwards.'

'Known what about her?'

'That, well — ' he handed Kate a glass of wine, having waited until they were eating their Chinese take-away before mentioning the incident — 'that you're sort of acting as her minder.'

'Who said so?' The prior warmth between them had promptly chilled. 'Who was it?'

'A phone call from some nob at the Yard.'

'Hammond, presumably. Or did he put his toady Barker on to it?'

'Hammond.' He hadn't expected her to be so instantly sensitive, seeing himself as the aggrieved party here, not Kate. 'Hang about, love. Until today, I knew nothing — '

'Fine.' She nodded, swallowing wine. 'So let's keep it that way.'

'Sure. Terrific. Except — '

'Except nothing! Forget it!' Then, thumping down her glass: 'Bloody Hammond! Bloody police! Bloody hierarchy! Bloody — '

'Listen — '

'Taff, I was determined not to involve you in any way at all. Nothing! Least of all that crass FAME story! Now here's bloody Hammond doing it for me!'

'Hardly.'

'He's leaning on you to lean on me!'

'He's not!'

Taff hadn't intended to get into a fight about it. They had enough tensions over where they were going to live without rowing over their blooming jobs. Yet, as usual, what a turn-on to see her getting all riled up like this, her face flushed, her eyes blazing . . . Absurdly perverse that the more heat between them, the more he wanted her. Could it, he wondered ruefully, be a trait special to coppers, notorious as the worst group for wife-beating?

'I told Hammond,' he said. 'Twice I said it to him. No way do I have any influence on my fiancée and her work.'

'Except that you *do*!' She was shaking her head, but more in irony than accusation. 'You just did: now that I know the bastard's leaning on you, I'll — well, at the very least

I'll have to tell Lawrence Cawley to put someone else on to it instead of me.'

'No way.' Taff gestured in rejection. 'Otherwise, Hammond will have won and we shall be reinforcing the damn hierarchical system.'

She thought it over, increasingly sexy as she scowled and shook her head before repeating her resentment. 'Bloody police!'

'OK, yes, fully agreed.' He sipped a toast to it before reaching out to her. 'Now let's hear the facts.'

Kate blinked at him. '*What?*'

'Look, if Hammond's going to try and lean on me, I need to know the vulnerable areas.'

She was still reluctant, repeating her determination to keep him totally *outside* her work. When she finally gave in, it was with the ironic revelation that in reality, until Bella had rung that morning to brief her about the Christmas-tree stunt, she hadn't seen or even heard from her for months.

'You're sure?'

'Would I lie to you?'

'Depends . . .'

'Taff, for God's sake!'

'Not out of deceit, but . . .'

'*What?*'

'I've been around you and your seedy line of business long enough now to clock a few of the tricks. And I have to say that, so far as I'm concerned, this one definitely has your signature on it.'

'This what? I don't know what you mean.' But she did. He could see it in her face as she pulled away to reach for the wine.

'The Christmas tree.'

'Ha! Taff, you're kidding!'

'More manager than minder, right? You want a good story—a good visual—exclusive to ITN. OK then, so you manufacture it. Or at the very least, inspire it.'

'You flatter me.' She smirked, the glass raised to hide her

eyes. 'Bella's plenty cute enough to dream up her own stunts. Plenty, plus some.'

'While along the way getting herself elected as a Brixton councillor.'

'Right!' Kate laughed, able to renew eye contact once again as she took his hand. 'There's nothing anyone can teach Bella Edwards about publicity. FAME is, quite literally, the spur.'

'Mandy baby, you are definitely the most beautiful thing this campaign has known in six long years.'

Bella Edwards chuckled, enthusiastically hugging Mandy Trotter to her plump bosom. There had been a time when, as a professional go-go dancer, Bella had been as slim and attractive as Mandy. Now, what with her appetite for Bacardi and spicy foods, she had fleshed up all round. True, her exceptional energy and drive were still there, fuelled indeed by her successes at the hustings. But those successes had also fuelled her appetites—for high living as well as high calories—balancing out the effects of energy burn-off.

As on all but the most informal occasions, Bella was clad for the benefit of her electoral supporters: purple tracksuit with the FAME logo emblazoned across front and back in letters of fire; pink high-heeled shoes, a pink wig and prominent pink spectacles completed the outfit, the startling effect further heightened by the contrast with the deep chocolate of her skin. The outfit was in effect a uniform, worn also by the half-dozen young black entertainers who made up the FAME team. They had also painted the FAME community centre in purple and pink stripes, as were their two transit vans, all of course enflamed with the FAME logo.

There was a chart-rating reggae celebrating FAME and a popular soul-styled Baptist hymn bewailing the injustices heaped on the ill-starred Aristotle. They held regular FAME discos for the young and FAME bingo evenings for the punters and FAME prayer meetings for the Baptists.

Over the years, the *Free Aristotle Macho Edwards* campaign
had proved a consistent growth industry, loyal black votes
and cash donations both testifying to the enduring appeal
of the cause.

'Let's damn-sure hope so,' Mandy sighed, pulling away
from the older woman's embrace, ''cos you gotta know,
Bella, it scares the living shit out of me.'

'Hush you, girl! You ain't going to get our man free if
you mess your mouth with tom talk like that.'

'You kidding?'

'Remember who we up against here. We can't hope to
win against Her Majesty's justice and the Westminster
slags without we have the Good Lord on our side. And,
Mandy girl, the Almighty ain't going to favour us if you go
foul-mouthing like that.'

'Straight up,' the younger woman nodded with a shrill
giggle, 'I won't even *think* wrong things. Ain't nothing going
to spoil the chance of getting Ari out that place.'

'Amen to that.'

'Amen and Alleluia.' She lit up a cigarette, drawing
deeply on it and wishing someone would give her a snort.
'So tell me how we go on from here.'

'Number one, I team you up with a lady friend of mine
from TV.'

'You kidding?'

'Ain't no way on this earth you simply going to walk into
Scotland Yard and tell them you was there and you *saw*
who really killed Arlene. No chance.'

'But holy shit, Mama, if they flash my face up there on
that tele screen, I'll end up stiffer than a pastor's plonker
at confirmation!'

'Your mouth, girl!' Then, seeing the depth of Mandy's
distress, she added less sharply: 'I ain't saying you'll be
on screen—leastways, not till we celebrating Ari's release
party. Like I say, this TV lady, she's a friend. Miss Katie
Lewis, right? Top reporter. Knows what's what and how
things got to be done when you dealing with the pigs.
Insurance, OK? When she's heard what you gonna say,

she'll tell us how best to package it as evidence for the lawyers.'

There was a tense pause before Mandy finally whispered: 'You got any sort of stuff here, honey?'

'Only when you seen my friend Katie Lewis. Ain't no way we going to risk you fouling up with her.'

Mandy grimaced, waving her urgently towards the telephone. 'So get on the horn, 'cos I tell you, I need something to hold me together.'

'Bloody . . .' she murmured yet again as they lay together, their bodies and their heartbeats still attuned in post-coital pleasures. 'Bloody police.'

'Again, lover, I agree with you. In fact—'

'The silly thing is, I wish you wouldn't.'

'Huh?'

'Agree all the time.'

'Ah.'

Keep on like this, he thought, and they could end up unable to make love *without* having a row!

'I mean, agree about the police being bloody. In a curious sort of way, I want you to stand up for them.'

'Ah.'

'I know all about their corruption and prejudice and chauvinism. I know how thick and pig-headed they can be. Yet the fact is, I want you to contradict it. It's like, I don't know, like wanting to believe in my blooming father when in reality I *knew* he was a disaster.'

Taff sighed, easing away from her to reach for a box of tissues. 'A good old love-hate thing, eh.'

'I suppose so.'

'Of course if we were to move out of town—get away from all these bent London Bobbies . . .'

'Hey, don't start on again about moving. Those tunnel-vision bosses of yours.'

'As a matter of fact, love, what with them and that call from Hammond and all the rest of the hassle, I've pretty well decided to . . .'

But it wasn't to be: the phone intervened to demand attention.

'Decided what?' Kate asked, catching his look as she reached out to answer it.

'It can wait until you've seen off that intruder.'

It turned out to be her ultimate master, the ITN newsdesk, ringing to let her know Bella Edwards had just telephoned for her to make contact pronto.

'Well, tough. She can wait until the morning.'

'That's down to you, Kate, but Madam FAME reckoned it's urgent.'

'Go on,' Taff called, clearing the remains of the takeaway as Kate rang off. 'You can't spend all night wondering.'

CHAPTER 2

'Katie baby!' Bella's embrace was humid and yeasty. 'If you ain't just the best friend a soul could wish!'

'You earn it, making people laugh the way you do.'

'Yeah?'

'You made my boyfriend's day with that tree stunt this morning.'

'What we need,' Bella snorted, 'is a wheeze or two out of the Lord Chancellor!'

Kate shook her head, turning to lock her car. 'So come on, what've you got that's so urgent?'

'The key, Katie baby, that's what. A key called Mandy Trotter who's guaranteed to unlock those old prison doors!' She led the way in from the street but paused in the apartment lobby. 'All along we've known about Mandy as a witness, but Ari flatly refused to have her put at risk.'

She pulled a face, spreading her arms in a gesture of frustration. 'What you gotta know about Ari, he ain't no hard-arsed businessman. Why, he's more like a father to his girls. Soft, understanding, protective. When he heard what Mandy seen, there was no way he was going to let her speak out. Told her, Mandy girl, you do what the pig's telling you: you keep quiet and you get the hell out of the country!'

The woman's eyes rolled white against her dark skin. 'Maybe she ain't the brightest kid on two feet. Maybe she don't have the wit except to do what he tell her. Anyway, she went. Took off to the Gulf with a favourite Arab daddy and only come back last summer. Then today she heard that on the radio about FAME and how Ari still locked up.'

She led Katie into the apartment to meet the taut black girl who stood by the window, her arms hugged tightly across her chest. Although she was no classic beauty, it was possible to see how her short upper lip, big eyes and retroussé nose could well offer an appealing vulnerability. The smile she flashed, although tense and lopsided, lit up her face with a childish charm.

'Bella says you ain't going to put me up on that screen. That right, Miss Lewis?'

'Not unless that's what you want.'

'All I want, ha, is to see Ari out the nick.' She had an affected manner of speech, punctuating her words with little ha-like gasps. 'Like I told Bella, I'll do whatever.'

Like commit perjury, Kate wondered.

'Right then, tell me what you saw. I know it was a long time ago. More than seven years. But . . .'

'Yesterday, ma'am. In my head, it's like it was yesterday, ha.' She paused to draw deeply on her cigarette before commencing. 'See, that poor kid Milt—er, Arlene Milton —she was my friend, know what I mean? We both worked for Ari, so we was mates. That night in August . . .'

'. . . I went round to fetch her. Usually, after we both got finished for the night, we'd go off for a drink at Leon's or one of the clubs. Anyway, as I reached the top of the stairs, I heard this noise. Like gasps it was, ha, gasps of pain.'

Mandy ran the tip of her tongue along her red-caked lips

and blinked in the bright glare of the TV-studio lights.
'Holy sugar, I ain't going to make it.'

'Hold it there, Mike.' Kate smiled in apology to the
cameraman as she moved to reassure the young black
woman. 'There's no hurry, Mandy. Take your time. It's
just that we have to tape a record, if only as an insurance.'

'Maybe, if I could, like, have a drink . . .' There was a
warning rumble from where Bella stood outside the pool of
light. 'Just mineral water, mama. Or fruit juice, whatever.'

Kate organized one, watching while she drank it down,
wondering just what the hell would be the outcome of it all.
For sure, on the face of it, the black girl's testimony could
hardly be ignored. But what about the legal establishment?
Would they find a way of discrediting it?

'OK then, ready to go on?' Pause. 'Once we get it taped,
you can have a real drink.'

'It's a deal. Where was I?'

Kate asked for playback and showed her the monitor.
The effect on Mandy was galvanic, bringing wild shrieks
at the sight of herself on screen. Fortunately, it seemed to
restore her resolve.

'I heard these gasps, ha, and also grunts and stuff like
that. OK, at first I didn't think too much of it. In our line
of business, you gotta provide for all sorts, ha. Also, Milt
being well trained—I mean a good performer, OK—them
gasps was most likely just part of the trick. So OK, I figured
it was just a late client and I'd best leave them to it. Even
when I hear her come on with this sort of stifled sream, I
thought it was all part of the trick. But just then I hear the
geezer start yelling at her. "You're a grass!" he says. "A
lousy copper's nark!" Then as he said it, I heard this sort
of slap and Milt yells out something awful. So after that, I
figured I'd best take a dekko.'

She paused, seemingly to muster her recollections. Yet,
watching her, Kate was struck by the stilted, almost theatrical style of her delivery. Not that that was so unusual, given
the studio atmosphere.

'I had a key, of course, on account of sometimes I had

to use the place for entertaining punters. So I unlocked the door and eased inside real cool. Like I'd figured, they was through in the bedroom. He's going on about her being a copper's nark again—accusing her, like—and poor Milt sobbing. Well, I'm wondering if I dare try for a look at him when he suddenly lurches across the bedroom. A mean, wiry little bastard he was, with hands like an ape and short-cropped gingery hair. And for sure, he was white, no question of that. Nor'd I see any sign of Ari being there. None. Just this whitey geezer.'

She paused to take another drink and light a cigarette before shaking her head. 'Sorry, Miss Lewis.'

'What happened then? Did he see you?'

'No. But it gave me God's own shock. Next thing I'm back out the place and off down the stairs quick as a flash. Time I got out down the street, I was still shook up and trembling, ha. Find a copper, that's what I kept thinking. But you know how it is: the pigs never give you any peace except the one time you really want them, ha. Then after a while I started thinking: Mandy you're a one-hundred-per-cent prat. Chances are he was just a punter what fancied a bit of aggro and if I got the Law charging up there, no way was Milt going to thank me for it. So—so, God forgive me, in the end I didn't do it. I went down the club, had a skinful and got stupid.'

Another pause and more headshaking before: 'By the time I got round there next day, Ari was doing his marbles 'cos she was out and he had a big-deal client lined up for her that evening. Of course, that was it. She never did show up, ha—not till they found her wrapped up in bin-liners down the building site.'

She paused to blow her nose, sniffing and scratching at her arms like a junky before calming down a bit. Kate let them keep taping until she managed to resume.

'OK, a couple of days after they found her, I managed to get meself along to the dicks on the case.' She guffawed in ridicule. 'They told me—would you believe it, the police told me they didn't want to know. Forget it, sweetheart, that's what this big plonker of a detective told me. We know it was Ari Edwards what done it. We also know about you —how you're on a probation order and one of Ari's stable. It's obvious you're just trying to alibi him 'cos he's your pimp, so just do yourself a favour, save us all a lot of grief and get lost.'

Pause for more headshaking and sighs of remorse before: 'When I went with Bella to see Ari in Brixton nick, he said the same thing—said how the pigs had stitched him up tighter than a vasectomy and the best thing I could do was forget what I'd seen and get lost. The further away, the better, that's what he said.'

She paused in apology, staring past Kate to where the older black woman stood listening. 'Bella got real mad at him, but Ari wouldn't budge. Kept ordering me to go and not come back.'

'Which she did, eh. Went off for an extended Gulf sabbatical.'

'So she claims, Jack, yes.'

'Ah.'

'I haven't had a chance to check her passport yet.'

'But you do have some doubts?'

Kate leaned across to press the video button. 'See what you think of her performance in front of the camera last night.'

They were surrounded by the VDUs, scanners, printers and other hi-tech wizardry with which Jack Walsh had filled his City office. In the few years since his retirement as a CID chiefie to become head of security with a merchant bank, Walsh had developed a web of contacts and information almost as extensive as the one he was supposed to have left behind him at the Yard. Shrewdly, Klein Holdings allowed him optimum funds with minimum accountability; so long as their tame spook continued to sniff out and deter frauds, both in-house and out, he could have *carte blanche*— and cheap at the price.

However, the opportunities which this status bestowed

on the man were unlikely to corrupt him. He was too canny and had seen far too much villainy in his life ever to get on that slope. What turned 'Foxy' Walsh on was the satisfaction of monitoring the City's commercial chicanery—of knowing who had pulled a million or two on this deal or that and just how close they'd had to sail to the wind to get away with it. In point of fact, he seldom used his knowledge to intervene in the shark pool; and whenever he did, no one knew it had been Walsh who'd blown the whistle.

'I've seen better witnesses,' he remarked as the tape finished. 'But not many as sexy as that. What a body!'

'Yes, well, thanks to romantic gentlemen like you, it's her most marketable asset. The question is, did you believe her?'

'I can certainly believe the bit about the murder team officer telling her to get lost.'

'That would have been DI Barker, recently made up to super.'

'Can't say I knew him,' Walsh grunted. 'Not like I did his guv'nor, Ted Hammond.'

'A climber, right?'

'Turd Hammond to all those close to him.' He nodded bleakly. 'A climber, an arse-licker. Hooked on rank.'

'Right.' Kate nodded, giving Foxy a grin. 'Which is basically why I'm here for advice. How do we get Mandy Trotter's evidence to the DPP without Hammond and Barker burying it en route?'

There was a lengthy pause, Walsh eyeing her laconically. However, when it came, his response took her by surprise. 'The bastard's guilty. You do realize that, don't you? Edwards beat her so bloody savagely that he finally managed to kill the poor kid. I was still at the Yard then and I heard enough behind the scenes to *know* he was guilty.'

She went to answer, but Walsh persisted bitterly. 'OK, like the Birmingham Six and the Guildford Four and Winston Silcot and all the bloody rest, it all happened before the Police and Criminal Evidence Act changed the rules. In those bad old days, a man with a conscience could still blurt it all out—confess his motive, name his accomplices, spill his guilt all over the interview room—and it would actually *mean* something. Not any more. Not with a sly, fee-happy lawyer sitting on his lips.'

'Look, Jack, I can understand your bitterness . . .'

'Have you any idea how many of my collars have been reversed because of PACE? Half a dozen! Solid, reliable, bang-to-rights convictions every one of them.' He gave an anguished grunt. 'A lawyer's charter, that's what PACE was.'

'None the less . . .'

'And now you're here asking me to help with another of them.'

'Not exactly.'

'He was guilty, I tell you.'

'Listen, this is nothing to do with PACE. This is fresh evidence. Mandy Trotter's a material witness who, if she'd been called by his defence, could very well have swung the verdict.'

'Bollocks.' The ex-chief-super shook his head in contempt. 'She wasn't called because she never saw a damn thing! She's just the latest in a long line of crafty gimmicks dreamed up by the pimp's wife. Damn it, that woman's even worse than Sonia Sutcliffe, no question. Councillor Bella Edwards, riding the hustings on the blood of her husband's victim!'

Kate paused to let him calm down while she reviewed her strategy. For all his noisy prejudice, she very much wanted Foxy with her on this one. Nor was it just for the wealth of his experience and contacts either, but through something akin almost to superstition. She was well aware what a father figure he'd become to Taff over their years together. And, for all the apects of him which she despised, Foxy's strength and force of personality held a deep attraction for her.

'What the hell are you smiling at, girl?'

She shrugged. 'You know I can't breathe a whisper about any of this one to Taff.' She wagged her head, swinging her blonde hair like they do in the shampoo ads. 'Otherwise it'd be easy: he'd watch over my every move, keep me on the strait and narrow. So I thought—well, naturally, I thought of Papa Walsh.'

'Ha!' But he was tickled by her audacity none the less. 'All right then, my first bit of advice is free: leave it totally alone.'

'Which you know very well I can't do. Even if I agreed about Mandy being another of Bella's tricks, it'd be more than my job's worth to say so. Besides, my editor would simply hand the story over to Desmond or someone else.' She gave him a gesture of mock helplessness. 'So you see, I'm stuck with it.'

The man's leathery face twisted with a grin which duly commuted into a rueful chuckle of capitulation. 'Which, since you're Taff's girl and hence sort of my responsibility, means I have no blooming option but to go along with it willy-nilly.'

He chuckled again, leaning across to give her a hug which he would have liked to make a whole lot more intimate than it was. 'Tell you one thing, girl, it won't cause me any grief to go a few rounds with Turd Hammond again.'

For all his promise and intelligence, David Roberts can display an uncompromising lack of tolerance for minor human failings in fellow officers. Although commendable in regard to more serious character defects, this lack of flexibility might represent a problem were he to achieve top-level seniority. One has to wonder whether any force as chronically starved of resources as is the Thames Valley could possibly live up to the standards which, to judge from his record hitherto, Roberts might expect of those under his command.

Taff heard the cough and pointedly heavy tread which signalled the return of Chiefie Marsh and moved back from the open personnel file on the desk. Whereas Ralph Marsh couldn't allow him official sight of the file's comments, he was happy to leave it wide open on his desk while he went for a timely leak midway through the interview.

'It could be there's a legacy of prejudice you'll have to

live down, David—assuming, of course, that you are am-
bitious for senior rank.' Pause. 'Are you?'

'I'm a bit on-off about it, sir.'

'Depending on?'

One answer, of course, was on how things happened to
be at home. But so what? There was hardly an officer in
the force without that problem.

'For one thing, sir, on how much pressure I get from
above.'

The chief blinked in open surprise. 'Lynn giving you a
hard time?'

'No, on the contrary, sir, she's most supportive.'

'Well then, unless you mean me . . .'

'From the Met, sir, not here.'

'Really?' He seemed even more surprised. But then of
course Hammond wouldn't actually have spread any
poison—not yet. That would only happen later on, if Taff
failed to comply or else attempted some sort of retaliation.
'You want to talk about it?'

'Only, sir, in so far as it undermines my respect for and
hence my loyalty to the force. The command structure
places a lot of power in the hands of senior ranks. Like all
power, it's open to abuse. If I was to gain promotion, I
would regard it as part of my duty to curtail such abuse
should I encounter it.'

'Ah.' The briefest of pauses. 'Quite right.'

'If that suggests an uncompromising lack of flexibility,
perhaps I should leave the force and start afresh elsewhere.'

'Now, now, lad . . .'

'All right, fine. But I would like it on record that any
intolerance on my part relates primarily to those with senior
rank. Unless those at the top are above reproach, they can
hardly . . .

'Yes, yes, David, spare us the polemic.' He conceded an
exaggerated wink, adding a brief note to the comments
section on Taff's file. 'I take it you've no formal complaint
to make about this alleged pressure from the Met.'

'I'll handle it my way, thanks, guv'nor.'

'Oh dear,' the chief groaned, waving him hurriedly out of his office. 'On past experience, I reckon we'd rather have the formal complaint.'

'By the way,' Taff added as he left, 'Commander Hammond asked me to pass on his best regards.'

'Terrific, Kate old love,' Lawrence Cawley drawled. 'Oscar quality.'

As editors went, Kate decided, he was undoubtedly the most ego-driven, irritating and pig-headed she'd ever had the misfortune to work with. Sly, devious, cunning and, as such, undeniably top-editor material; also loyal to the bosses, their whims and policies. But as for loyalty to his team, as for sympathy or even common courtesy, oh boy . . . !

'We taped it solely as a precaution—as a record in case the police try any tricks.'

'Ah.' He smirked at her, indicating the cassette. 'Well, you could hardly get more tricksie than this little lot. There's only one thing this tape tells us for certain.'

Kate knew this was a cue for one of his facetious little quips, but he had to be indulged. 'Go on.'

'Simply that, no matter how skilled when performing on her back, Amanda Trotter never went to drama school.'

'She wasn't *that* bad.' Pause. 'She was extremely nervous.'

'Most likely on some sort of gear and in need of a fix,' the editor remarked, 'making her all the more receptive to Bella's demands. Anything—lies, make-believe, perjury—anything to keep herself topped up.'

'You and Foxy Walsh make a right pair: racist, sexist . . .'

'Did I mention her colour? Did I?'

'You didn't need to, Lawrence.' She grimaced, tossing the cassette into the nearest waste-bin. 'Too bad.'

'Tut-tut, dear, such histrionics.' He got laboriously to his feet, moving to retrieve the tape and dust it clean of cigar ash. 'No matter how phoney she is, we run with it. Terrific stuff. Whores, torture, a vice-land murder, claims of a six-year injustice—all the ingredients. Of course we run with it, no holds barred.'

'That go for expenses, too?'

'Well, as always, only within reason. Did you have anything exceptional in mind?'

'There are going to be lawyers' fees.' She laughed. 'That goes without saying, I know, but everything with Bella has a way of escalating.' She paused for the editor's dour nod, then added: 'Also, I'd like Jack Walsh on board as a consultant.'

'Oh?' He sniffed. 'Advertising revenue's way down and you spring this on me.' He pulled a face, eyeing her askance. 'May I ask what's wrong with your in-house consultant?'

'No, you may not!' Then, pre-empting any retort: 'Taff's my fiancé, OK?'

'Well, exactly! So we can pay him his consultancy fee via you. Keep it all in the family, all nice and discreet, all—'

'*No!*' Given the hundreds of retired policemen ready to sell their souls to get on the media payroll, the editor would obviously far prefer to hire a serving chief inspector. 'The fact is, Jack Walsh probably has far better resources than Taff; also he won't be betraying the terms of his employment.'

Cawley gave her an elaborate bow, acknowledging the finality of her tone. Not that the editor was beaten, of course, merely biding his time.

Mandy Trotter, whatever stimulants she had resorted to after the studio recording, looked in terrible shape when Kate called for her shortly before midday. Racked with the shakes, her skin grey and lifeless, dark glasses concealing her puffy eyes.

She apologized, trying to explain it as a booze hangover. Booze with additives, Kate concluded, offering to postpone their appointment with the Police Complaints Authority. To her credit, however, Mandy insisted they go through with it. So she was scared—so what? No chance of her getting any less scared by putting it off. Best to get on down there and get the thing over.

The ITN lawyer Kate had brought along was so subdued that Mandy hardly seemed to notice him as they got into the car. She waved a hand vaguely as Kate attempted introductions, then relapsed into something like a coma as the car moved off.

'You sure you're in a state to remember it all in as much detail as you did last night?'

'Like I said, ha, it's burned into my skull like it was yesterday.'

'The PCA may want to tape you, much like we did last night. OK?'

'In any event,' the lawyer murmured apologetically, 'they'll take down a full witness statement from you.'

It had been Jack Walsh's advice to go to the Police Complaints Authority. Although the PCA could very well take longer to get things moving, its independence from the police made it a far safer bet than either the Yard's C-Ten or their Complaints Investigation Bureau.

As it turned out, there was one unforeseen drawback about the Authority, but it only emerged after their arrival at the offices in Great George Street—appropriately if ironically sited midway between Scotland Yard and Downing Street. When making the appointment, Kate had merely said it was for a Miss Amanda Trotter with allegations of CID irregularities during a murder investigation in the mid-'eighties. The problem emerged the moment the name Aristotle Edwards was mentioned.

'Mrs Bella Edwards is no stranger to the PCA.' The interviewer was a rather grand lady with a double-barrelled name and a head that cried out for a tiara; certainly nothing Left-wing or anti-Establishment there, Kate decided. She had crossed to usher them into her office, but now remained standing in mid-room. 'You may not be aware, Miss Lewis, but since last year we have adopted a policy of referring Councillor Edwards and her people elsewhere.'

'As you can see, Miss Trotter is here with a solicitor and myself, not with Mrs Edwards.'

'Well, naturally she knew better than to come.'

'Excuse me,' the ITN lawyer intervened smoothly, 'but might we perhaps hear what prompted this policy?'

'Nothing improper on the part of the Authority, I assure you. The plain fact is that, over the years Mrs Edwards and her various supporters have lodged numerous complaints with us. Although all have been investigated at considerable length and expense, not one of them has proved valid.' She crossed her arms, continuing to stand her ground. 'The Authority is chronically underfunded to deal with the huge volume of complaints it receives. Priorities have to be applied. Moreover, our credibility is vulnerable to frivolous complaints. Our past efforts to assist Councillor Edwards have—have forced this policy on us.'

'Hey,' Mandy remarked in sudden animation, 'what's the hold-up, ha? Why all the gab?' She still had the shades on, her hands clasped tightly in front of her.

'Take our word for it,' Kate put in quickly, 'Miss Trotter is *not* one of the FAME team.' Briefly she outlined Mandy's evidence and the reason for the seven-year delay over coming forward. She also handed over a copy of their video recording of the previous evening. She would have liked to offer some documentary authentication, but Mandy seemed to have nothing: no driving licence, tax coding, DSS number or rent book, not even credit cards—nor, unfortunately, her passport. Ironic how those in the most intimate profession tended to be among the most anonymous and impersonal.

'And the nature of her complaint against the police?' The PCA woman listened while Kate told how Mandy's attempt to give her evidence had met with flat rejection, then she asked: 'Precise date and name of officer?'

'On or about July the tenth, 1985. She gave a verbal statement to the number-two on the murder squad, Detective-Inspector Alec Barker.'

For a long moment the PCA woman remained motionless, reluctance etched across her fine aristocratic features. Finally she turned and, eyeing the tape cassette, stalked round behind her desk. She gestured for Mandy and the lawyer to sit opposite her, then beamed Kate a false smile.

'While I can well appreciate ITN's proprietorial interest in these proceedings, Miss Lewis, I must insist you withdraw at this point. Any allegations of police malpractice which we decide to investigate become, in effect, *sub judice*.'

CHAPTER 3

'Listen Terry, me and my corporate employers don't give a monkey's toss whether it's one of Bella's tricks or not. Either way, it could still be strong enough to get the case reopened.'

There was a pause, the caller and Terry both breathing deeply. Mandy Trotter was a development which they could very readily have done without. Thanks to Bella Edwards and her FAME campaign, neither had been able to bury it and forget the nightmare. Instead, they had had six years of reminders, each bringing a chill breeze of fear which now, thanks to the advent of Mandy Trotter, was suddenly a storm.

'Is that what the Law's saying?'

'Never mind who's saying it? That's how it is. She's ready to go in the witness-box and swear she was there. She's given a fair description of you and she claims she saw you having a go at her mate Arlene. She says she heard you telling her she was a copper's nark and hoofing the life out of her.'

'Copper's nark . . . ?'

'That's right, Terry. Ring a bell, does it? Is that what you really did say?'

'How should I know? All them years ago! So who the hell is this Trotter cow?'

'She's a tom.'

'Aren't they all!'

'Used to be one of Ari's girls, so the man said.'

'Which man, Alan. Who you on about?'

'The man who belled me. Name of Barker, OK? Remember him from the trial, do you? Well he's just read her sing-song and he's telling us to get some action going or else!'

'Else what, for Christ's sake, else what?'

'Else you and him could go down the pan, that's what!' Another pause, the storm gusting up to hurricane force. 'Action?'

'She has to go, OK. Nothing else for it.'

'Get stuffed!'

'I will ask you just once, on behalf of my corporate employers, whether you really want to repeat that.' Pause. 'Now then, it ain't got to be no accident like falling under a train or something like that. She's got to *disappear*. Totally. It's got to look like she's had second thoughts, lost her bottle and done a runner, OK?'

'Listen, Alan, listen, this is crazy! It's just another stupid trick! Just Bitch Bella's latest—'

'I told you, whether it is or not don't matter! What matters is that this slag Trotter's saying things which can get the whole can of worms opened up again. And that, Terry mate, is your misfortune and her mistake. Get it?'

Yet another pause, long and tense, before: 'So where do I find her?'

'Ah, well, that's not so easy either. Seems the only address given on her statement was care of ITN.'

'Oh, that's stunning, that is! Don't know what she looks like, don't know where she lives. Nothing except that seven years ago she could have been one of Ari's toms!'

'She's black, according to the man.'

'Great! That really narrows it down!'

'With ITN involved, you can be sure Kate Lewis'll be on it. Also, like you say, Bella's got to be involved behind the scenes.'

'So?'

'So that's two possible leads for you to get after.'

PROSECUTOR: Mr Edwards, you've been at pains to try and tell the court what prestigious clients Arlene Milton entertained, yes?

ARISTOTLE EDWARDS: You're right, sir, she did. Top-drawer people, OK. People I want to get right here in the court. People like Sir William . . .

JUDGE: That will do, Edwards. I have already ruled on that issue.

PROS: Your Honour, I'm obliged. Top-drawer people, as you say, Mr Edwards. People with influence, people with money. Yes?

Taff grunted with irritation as the telephone interrupted yet again. He laid the trial transcript aside, apologized to the caller that he had no idea when Kate would be back, rang off and switched the machine on to answer phone. Then, humming to himself, he poured a beer and went back to the cross-examination.

AE: Damn right they had influence, sir.

PROS: And as such, people who would most certainly be vulnerable to blackmail.

AE: No, sir. That was part of the deal. No risk for the client.

PROS: What deal? Are you saying you were operating on behalf of some parent organization?

AE: No, sir.

PROS: The jury has already heard how the majority of Arlene Milton's clients were drawn from customers at Blandells Casino. Did you have some sort of deal with the management of Blandells?

AE: No, sir, I was simply talking about the deal with the client.

PROS: The client. Really? Perhaps we could just get this fully clear. Are you telling the jury you were personally acquainted with all these top-drawer clients? They contacted you direct for appointments to enjoy the favours of the late Arlene Milton, yes? Is that what these highly esteemed clients would tell us if you were allowed to sub-pœna them to give evidence? Speak up, Mr Edwards, so the jury can hear you.

AE: Yes, sir.

PROS: Well now, I put it to you that your clients were not only vulnerable to blackmail but were in fact exposed to blackmail.

AE: Lies. Who says so?

PROS: I'm suggesting to you, Mr Edwards, that you had a camera concealed in the room where Arlene Milton entertained these top-drawer clients.

AE: No.

PROS: A camera concealed for the obvious purposes of blackmail.

AE: No.

DEFENCE: Your Honour, may we know if the Crown intends to substantiate this line of suggestion?

JUDGE: Mr Richardson?

PROS: Your Honour, yes. I would like to re-introduce Exhibit C-4. Namely, photographs which the Crown claim were taken by this concealed camera. I would remind the jury that these photographs were found by the police hidden at the accused's address.

AE: Like hell they was!

JUDGE: That will do, Edwards.

AE: Sir, they was planted.

JUDGE: Enough, I said. Yes, Mr Richardson?

PROS: Perhaps Your Honour would care to re-examine them.

JUDGE: Pass them up then. Thank you. Members of the jury, you will recall that Detective-Inspector Barker stated in evidence that he found these photographs when searching the accused's premises in Notting Hill. However, you just heard Mr Edwards claim with some force that they were planted in his apartment. You should give consideration to that claim when examining this exhibit.

PROS: I'm obliged, Your Honour. Mr Edwards, is the room

which is shown in these photographs the one which Arlene Milton used to entertain her clients?

AE: So?

PROS: Look at the two pictures marked C-4-D and C-4-E. Thank you. One of the women shown in them is Arlene. Can you identify the other women visible in those two pictures? The one holding a camera?

AE: No, sir.

PROS: No? Are you quite certain?

AE: Hundred per cent certain.

PROS: Isn't it correct that her name is Janine McKane, an erstwhile employee of Blandells casino?

AE: Don't know her, sir.

PROS: And that her purpose in visiting Arlene was to arrange to photograph Arlene's clients with the camera shown here so that the pair of them could then attempt blackmail on their own behalf?

AE: Man, how should I know?

PROS: You would know, Mr Edwards, because it was when you found out about her blackmail plan with Janine McKane that you killed Arlene Milton.

AE: No!

PROS: Isn't that the reason you were beating her so brutally?

DEF: Your Honour, this is flagrant speculation. Since me friend failed to produce this mysterious Janine McKane to give evidence to the jury . . .

Taff heard Kate's key in the door and moved to conceal the transcript. Then he thought better of it and instead waved it at her as she walked into the room.

'Hot reading material you left me.'

'Damned nosey copper!' She dived to retrieve it, struggling for possession when he hung on. 'Let go!'

'You're kidding! Lurid stuff—sex, blackmail . . .' He ducked and let go of it as she swung at him. 'What's wrong?'

'I *told* you—I don't want you involved!'

'Just skimming through the transcript doesn't involve

me.' Then, grinning: 'To quote the poet: *FAME is a food that dead men eat; I have no stomach for such meat.*'

She moved away, giving him an exaggerated glare. 'Prying into my stuff . . .'

'Which you'd left bang in the middle of the table . . . I mean, you'd obviously left it out for me to read.'

'Uh-huh . . .'

There was a pause, Kate huffing through to the bedroom while Taff went to the kitchen and poured her a drink.

'So come on then,' she asked, once she'd changed her clothes and calmed down. 'What do you think?'

'From what little I read of Ari's cross-examination, it's certainly strong meat.'

'Did you read all that about the confession?'

'Not yet. Only the mysterious Janine McKane.'

'Ah—the one in the photograph—the alleged accomplice blackmailer.'

'Which, according to the Crown, was the prime motive for the killing.'

'Hotly denied, of course.'

'Of course. Mind you, the Crown had problems if they hadn't even managed to find this girl Janine and call her as a witness.'

'Right. Their main corroboration about her, apart from the photographs, came from the two confessions.'

'Two?'

'One which DI Barker claimed to have got when he first arrested Ari, the other a so-called prison-yard confession.'

'To a fellow remand prisoner, huh?'

'Called Alfred John Small.'

While they talked, Taff had eased round to retrieve the transcript, then start leafing casually through it. 'Alfred Small . . .'

'Damn you, give it back!'

'Why? Look at it as a busman's holiday.' He laughed. 'I'm your in-house armchair detective.'

Which, had she been strictly honest with herself, could

perhaps have accounted for her carelessness in leaving it
around for him to find.

'Well, I suppose . . .'

'Good.' He sat down and reached for his glass, then
added: 'As for you, mistress—promise you won't let Bella
involve you in anything dicey.'

'Ha. With Bella everything's dicey—and noisy and
cheeky and exotic. Carnival time, baby!'

Taff pulled a face, knowing exactly what she meant and
just as uneasy with it. Carnival time: exotic anarchy,
erotic ebullience, chaotic hedonism—all dimensions which,
although they might appeal at an atavistic level, were alien
to the ordered and orderly priorities of a white Caucasian
policeman. 'Well, at least promise you'll keep Foxy Walsh
in the picture.'

'Chaperon, eh, baby?'

'If not for the carnival, certainly for when the Met get
after you—chaperon, chastity belt, body armour, the lot!'

Carnival was Kate's first thought when she arrived at the
candy-striped FAME community centre next morning. As
well as a DoE conversion grant and local-authority funding,
the centre also received support from registered charities
such as the Christian Urban Fund. Right now, however, the
entire converted warehouse was throbbing with amplified
reggae as a troop of dancers in Afro-Caribbean costumes
demonstrated a skilled if suggestive routine to the high
delight of a class of a hundred or so black youngsters.

'Katie baby!' Bella emerged from among a throng of
parents at the far end to plunge the ITN reporter enthusiastically into her embrace. 'Welcome to FAME land.' She
tried to pull her towards the stage. 'Come and join them.
You'll look terrific up there. Hey, kids, get a breeze of our
dinky new star!'

'Leave it out, will you, Bella, I'm strictly waltz and
tango.' She nodded at the grinning youngsters. 'Are these
all recruits?'

'Hell no! At most maybe one or two going to make the

team.' She gave a shrill laugh, hugging Kate. ''Cepting we ain't going to need no team—not any more—not now you and Mandy about to spring our boy to freedom.'

Kate shook her head, but before she could voice any caution, Bella was dragging her across to meet a tall, flashily-dressed man joking with a couple of the prettier girls in the audience. A pimp, was Kate's first thought, hoping to extend his stable.

'Randi, over here and meet sister Katie.' Then, more sharply when the man paused for a parting word with the girls: 'Katie Lewis of ITN, OK!'

That got him moving—with a spring and a bound which ended in a mock bow deep to the ground. 'Miss Lewis, Randi Dubois. I'm just totally hooked on your show.'

'Don't lark about here, Randi.' Bella turned, resuming to Kate in explanation. 'Randi's a lawyer. Best I ever found.' She fended him off as he tried to goose her. 'I said lawyer, you flake, not hanky-panky man.'

Randi stopped grinning and donned a pair of heavy spectacles to peer solemnly at Kate. 'See, ma'am, it's the crazy magic of this place. Each time I come here it hits me like I just walked into a steamy great orchid house.'

'If that's what turns you on, Mr Dubois.'

'Kate, supposing you call me Randi. We're going to have to skip all the formal stuff if we're working together.'

Kate turned in surprise to Bella, who nodded, seemingly unabashed. 'Randi's taking on Mandy's case.'

'Mandy and Ari together,' the lawyer put in firmly. Then, raising his hands Frank Bruno style, he added: 'Fighter for the cause of freedom, at your service!'

Kate blinked, switching to the role of calculator. She didn't mind losing the ITN lawyer who'd seen Mandy through the Police Complaints Authority. In fact it was a relief, the man being far too reserved and British for a story like this one—closer to funeral than carnival. However, as usual, there could be huge problems with that mean old racist editor of hers.

'One small technicality, Randi: it'll ease the payment

situation if you can let us have an advance note of your rates. OK?'

Randi gave an ingenuous snort, waving his hands as if to imply that fees were irrelevant since fighters for the cause of freedom usually expected to fight for free.

As it turned out, of course, Lawrence Cawley contradicted Kate's expectations when she took Randi round to the ITN newsroom. The black lawyer's breezy flamboyance seemed to delight the editor, his enthusiasm remaining undimmed even over the issue of fees.

'It'll do those smug ITN lawyers of ours a power of good to have a bit of exotic competition,' he chuckled once Kate had shunted Randi off to watch a copy of Mandy'd tape. 'Truly charismatic.'

'Lawrence, me old soul mate, aren't you going a little bit over the top here?'

'Listen, darling, Randi's manna from heaven: the perfect chocolate topping to the year's most fruity story.'

'Barker's what?!'

'Waiting in your office, sir.' Sergeant Warboys shook his head, his hands spread in apology. 'He said it was important. I knew you'd be in fairly soon.'

'I do have a car-phone.'

'I got an engaged tone, sir. Sorry.'

Taff shrugged, realizing the sergeant could hardly have known this particular Yard superintendent was about the last person Taff would have wanted shown into his office.

'Surprise call, Mr Barker.'

'I happened to be in the area and wanted a word.' The super was a large, bucolic, jovial-looking man in his late fifties, doubtless relieved to have made it to the rank of super before retirement. He looked ill at ease, forcing a grin as he shook Taff's hand. 'I'd have preferred it if we could have met up for lunch but . . .'

'But after my call from Mr Hammond, you knew I wouldn't go for it.'

'Listen, Ted's not an easy man to talk to. Stiff and self-important. Rank's gone to his head, huh. Whatever he said, you don't want to let it bug you.'

'Oh, but it did, sir. So do you. So I'll repeat what I told him, just the once, and then you can go.'

'Don't bother. I know what you told him.'

'Good. Well then, since we're releasing the annual crime figures today and also—'

'At the very least, Roberts, do me the courtesy to hear me out.' He was flushed and tense now, fists clenched as he scowled across at him.

Taff took off his watch and laid it on the desk. 'You have five minutes. And don't waste any of it singing me the *PACE of Change Blues*, OK?'

'They said you were a cocky bastard.'

'Look, suppose we get this clear: there is no way I want anything to do with you or with the Ari Edwards case or the Yard or *anything* other than the job I'm trying to do here. I've had more than enough hassle with the Met over the last few years; I just want to keep my nose clean and, like you, get on with earning my promotion.'

'Fine, mate, fine.' The man's heavy jowl bobbed up and down. 'We speak the same language—same hopes, same frustrations, both paddling the same canoe. You know what it's like to collar a felon for a really nasty bit of villainy and have him sing his head off with all the details of what he did and why he did it, only to change his tune the moment his brief's come in and had a go at him. You know that feeling. There ain't a single DC and upwards who doesn't know that feeling.'

He paused, his pouchy eyes fixed on Taff for the response he so keenly sought. 'The thing about the Edwards case, it wasn't just the forensic evidence and those two confessions and the tom witness and all the rest. The thing was, we *knew* it was him for certain long before any of that. Had the word, didn't we. Had it from a one-hundred-per-cent reliable snout.'

Of course, Taff thought, his face a mask, the good old dependable snout. Like the shoot-to-kill deaths in Northern

Ireland, like the Guildford bombers, like so many, many others; in fact, the majority of successful clear-ups depended on information received—the crucial inside lead—out of spite or envy or vengeance or else just plain greed. But as for ever taking the informant as one-hundred-per-cent reliable? God forbid.

'We couldn't put him in the witness-box, of course. Well, anyway, what with all the other evidence, there was no need. We had a cast-iron case, no problem.'

Taff laid a finger on his watch. 'The point being?'

'The point being that it was a vile, disgusting murder and we *know* it was Ari Edwards who did it. Our consciences are totally clear; justice was done. There is nothing whatso-ever to be served by reopening the case. His wife knows he's guilty same as we do; all she wants is the FAME publicity to boost her political ambitions. Westminster, right. So you see, there's absolutely no point at all in reopening the whole ugly business.'

Ah, but ugly for whom, Taff wondered: for just you and Hammond? Or is there pressure from all those 'top-drawer' Establishment customers sensitive about their moment of bimbo? He held up the watch, but the superintendent pressed angrily on.

'It was a vile crime and we managed to get our convic-tion, Roberts.' He waved the watch aside, jabbing a finger at Taff. 'Just like you did with that filthy little pervert Leonard Snow. You knew he was guilty, you knew how many years he'd been banging those poor little kids. You knew he had to be stopped, so you did the business and you stopped him. Justice, OK. And there's no way you'd want to see the Snow case reopened, any more than we want the Edwards case reopened.'

Taff was on his feet now and striding round to get him out. But Barker moved quickly to block the way before he could open the office door. 'In case Commander Hammond didn't make himself fully clear, I'm here to give it you straight. You tell your Miss Lewis she's out of order with that phoney witness Mandy Trotter. Way out of order.'

'Very well then, sir, go ahead and report her to the Press Council. Do her for accessory to false testimony or aiding and abetting perjury or whatever you like! It's your problem, not mine. I don't have any control over what Kate Lewis does. None at all.'

'Then you'd better start, Roberts, you'd better start. Otherwise you could find yourself getting a taste of what we're getting. It's no joke, I tell you, having your past dug over!'

The queue outside HM Prison Wormwood Scrubs was shorter than usual. Being not yet midday, there were a few still waiting for morning visitors or else families who had arrived extra early for the afternoon session. Although it was by no means Kate's first such visit, she still found it a disturbing experience. She could sense so much pent-up tension in those around her in the queue. For the majority, be they parents, wives or children, their visit would be a high point of renewal, yet one tinged with shame and humiliation.

For her part, Bella was far from her usual jazzy self, failing to respond to the rattle of Randi's repartee, blowing her nose, coughing and fiddling with the hem of her orange silk jacket. For once, she had forsaken the FAME tracksuit, tersely explaining that the one time she had worn it for a visit, the prison officers had retaliated with everything bar a full strip search.

To Kate's relief, as they finally got inside the massive walls to be vetted at the reception counter, Randi produced his lawyer's credentials, then got all legalistic with the desk officer about letting in his ITN sponsor. Even so, the officer insisted on phoning some higher authority before writing out an access pass for Kate.

Annoyingly, although she got her mini tape-recorder through the metal detector, the officer on handbag checks was emphatic about its temporary removal. 'Regulations, madam.'

The visiting hall, given the number of people crowded at

its fifty or so tables, was amazingly quiet. Later, with the influx of children during the afternoon session, it would become far more raucous. But now the talk was hushed and intimate beneath the pall of cigarette smoke.

They had to wait all of ten minutes before Ari was produced, Bella increasingly nervous and even Randi subdued by the dour atmosphere in the place. There was nothing dour about Ari Edwards, however. The moment he was escorted in, Kate knew it must be him: grinning and waving, his dark face seeming to glisten with excitement, even his prison tunic tarted up with a plastic flower pinned to the lapel.

'Look at her!' he exclaimed, heaving the squawking Bella off her feet in a massive hug before turning to blow Kate a kiss across the table and go through the hand-slap ritual with Randi Dubois. 'Baby, this here's some party we got going. Where's the bubbly and cigars? Don't tell me you let them greedy screws grab the lot!'

It was a surprise to find him so relaxed and ready with the laughs. Surely, Kate thought, the six years in the Scrubs must have changed him: six years of containment and oppression, his horizons narrowed to the grimy walls of the cell block, his social contacts limited to defeated fellow cons and sullen officers, scope for his mind to dwell on little else but the bitter injustice of his imprisonment or else the horror of his crime—assuming it was indeed, as the Crown had claimed, due to his vicious brutality that poor Arlene Milton had died.

Certainly, six years was going to be merely the slim end of a sentence for such a savage murder, with little prospect of his even being re-categorized down from A for a year or two. But looking at the big amiable goof of a man—watching him strike up an instant rapport with the black lawyer while teasing his tubby wife and joking with Miss Media Lewis—witnessing such warm joviality, Kate found it hard indeed to imagine him resorting to such murderous violence.

'That's right,' Bella said, seemingly reading Kate's

thoughts, 'take a good look at him, look at the man they said did those wicked things. He look a devil to you? He look like a monster?' Then, when Kate shook her head: 'Of course he don't! This here's my baby. This here's the overgrown totty me and the FAME team and the whole Brixton community been fighting for all these years.'

She turned to hug him, laughing shrilly as she kissed his cheek. 'This here's the daddy you two folks going to win justice for, huh!'

The remark seemed to surprise and even alarm her husband. Frowning, he listened closely as Bella launched in about the exciting new evidence, submitted via the PCA, from the first real witness to speak out on his behalf.

'I know, baby,' she concluded, 'I know what you said to her when you was on remand—telling her to get out the country for her own sweet good, but—'

'Told who, Bella?'

'Why, little Mandy Trotter, of course.'

'*Mandy?*' His fists crashed on to the table. 'God's sake, I told you!'

'Sure, honey, I know, I know. But see, when she heard how you was still locked up in here, the kid was just—why, she was just beside herself—'

'So horray, let her weep for me! But nothing else for Christ's sake!'

'Our one and only witness!'

'You want that kid dead, Bella? That what you're after?' He was sweating freely now, his clenched fists pounding on the table. 'Sure as God, that's what she'll be if you make her go through with this crap!'

'Ari my man,' Randi Dubois put in soothingly, 'you listen to me now. Miss Trotter's given her evidence already. She registered it with the Complaints Authority who have now formally passed it to the Department of Public Prosecutions. It's in process. The legal machine is rolling. That means, for better or worse, there is no way anyone can stop it. Not now.'

There was a heavy pause before the prisoner at last

nodded his head, but in grim irony as much as understanding. 'Sure, fella, sure. It's rolling so fast it's already rolled into this here prison.'

'In here, honey?'

Ari Edwards swung with a curt nod to his wife. 'Doesn't take long to get messages delivered inside. Phone call to a bent screw, the screw to one of the heavy mob; and I get the word, OK, along with a touch of body language to show they mean business.'

'They roughed you up?'

'Just a taster.' He indicated his back and shoulders. 'Nothing broken—not yet.' He gestured in renewed irony to the lawyer. 'Man, I had no notion what the hell they was on about: telling me to lay off, quit rocking the boat, or else.' He resumed to Bella, but now in open rebuke. 'I sure as hell know now! You geed up that kid Mandy— one and only witness, all that crap—and now the legal machine's a-rolling! Oh boy!'

'Ari, I swear to God—'

'Just—Bella, if you want to help me like you keep saying —just fucking lay off!'

CHAPTER 4

The queue outside was far longer by the time they left the prison, mostly wives and children waiting in a chilled, straggling line between the towering prison wall and the windows of the officers' club.

The three walked in silence to the car park. All were chastened by the grim ethos of the place but more so by the violent intimidation that their precious *due legal process* had unleashed on Ari Edwards.

It was unlikely, even had she been watching out for anyone following them, that Kate would have noticed the grubby Range-Rover which nosed out from the kerb as she pulled into Du Cane Road.

'Could it possibly have been a coincidence?' she asked, glancing at Bella in the passenger seat beside her. 'I mean, whoever it is threatening Ari, how on earth could they have known about Mandy going to the Complaints Authority?' Then, when Bella responded with little more than a dour shrug, she added: 'Surely the PCA doesn't leak things, nor does the Director of Public Prosecutions.'

'Further investigations,' Randi remarked from the back seat. 'The DPP simply copies the evidence to the Yard with a request for further investigations.'

'By who? Barker and Hammond, for Pete's sake?'

'Since Barker's implicated with irregularities, they should have handed it to the Yard's complaints bureau.' He grunted in irony. 'Who no doubt then confronted Barker with Mandy Trotter's statement. Get the picture?'

Kate nodded, oppressed as much by their shared responsibility as by the sinister implications.

'So—so whatever do we do now?' There was a pause, the other two both seemingly perplexed by her question. 'We can't just ignore it.'

'Ignore what?'

'The threat to your husband.' Kate hooted as a taxi cut in ahead of her. 'I mean, presumably we . . .'

'We what?'

'Surely it's obvious: we get Mandy to withdraw her evidence.'

'Withdraw?' Bella was openly shocked. 'The first and only witness?'

'Not only that,' the lawyer cut in. 'We'd be giving in to threats.'

Kate went to argue, but he persisted, his voice shrill with conviction. 'Hell, that's not the road to justice. My whole life I've been up against the Establishment and fighting their damned system. Be sure, the one thing I've learnt is never to back down. Threats from the Bar Council, racist taunting, fire-bombings, no matter what, you just never let them scare you off. Never.'

'But—' Kate gestured in uncertainty—'I mean, suppose

they *kill* him?' She glanced sharply at Bella. 'You want to risk that?'

'Of course I don't. But, so help me, I want him *out*. I want a retrial and his name cleared!'

'There are ways,' the lawyer put in quickly, 'ways of securing his safety. Even inside prison, there are ways.'

'You mean, rule forty-three?' Kate asked. 'Get him into solitary like the sex offenders?' She could imagine the jokey, gregarious Ari being really turned on by that.

'That's how it is.' The lawyer shrugged. 'So it's tough, but look how high the stakes are.'

Agreed, Kate thought, and not only Ari's freedom at stake but the Dubois reputation as a lawyer, Bella's ambitions as a politician—even mine as a flaming scoop-hunter!

Mandy may have been anonymous in terms of her documentation, but the frilly possessions crammed into the Bayswater flat which Bella had rented as a hideaway sang out to Kate as one huge attempt at self-expression—most probably, in view of the mounds of Teddies, bunnies and other over-stuffed toys, to do with an arrested childhood. Mandy was thrilled to show them off, skipping elf-like between the taffeta and satin, the china ornaments and glassware, while introducing them to her more special cuddlies which she duly plonked on their laps while she prepared them lunch-time tea.

She was a different person in the safe seclusion of the flat, twee and childlike, cooing and twittering, with no hint of the shakes or a hangover any more than of the tense, strung-out witness who had testified in front of the studio cameras. She greeted Randi without at first seeming to register that he was a lawyer, handing him the most imposing of the Teddies which, she exclaimed, was called Ari-Bear after guess who. If she was high on anything, Kate could detect no tell-tale signs of dilated pupils or slurred speech. On the contrary, she was the epitome of the houseproud hostess.

Only when Randi tried to steer the talk around to her

evidence did the mask—or else the fantasy—start to slip. 'Can't we forget all that stuff, ha? Here, just be Daddy and cut the cake. Let's everyone enjoy the party, OK?'

'Sure, honey, it's all delicious. But we've come here to go through this witness statement with you.' He pulled it from his jacket. 'There's a whole lot of stuff in here I need to check out.'

'Check *shit!*' Then, instantly contrite: 'Sorry, Bella, sorry, Miss Lewis. Sometimes—I don't know—sometimes the devil gets a hold of my tongue. More tea, mama?'

If the lawyer was at all put out by his client's outburst, he gave no hint of it, instead calmly holding out his cup for a refill before asking: 'How come so many differences between what you said on Miss Lewis's video tape and what's here in the PCA statement?'

'Differences?' Yet even now she sought to evade it, turning to offer petits fours to Kate and Bella and the Teddies.

'You put in far more detail on the tape. For instance, in the statement, you missed out the whole thing about trying to find a policeman.'

'OK, man! So what? The way that godalmighty PCA bitch treated me, I could have forgot my fucking name!' She paused with a sob to snatch Ari-Bear away from him and hug it close. 'Lousy bitch!'

'The Complaints Authority woman was suspicious about Mandy,' Kate told the lawyer. 'Over the years, they've managed to lose patience over the succession of complaints from the FAME team.'

Bella gestured in mock outrage, but the younger woman stormed in first. 'Bitch kept on and on and on at me, ha! Picking on this and that, having me repeat things, asking over and over how come I'd left it so long, where'd I been the last six years, all that shit. Cow had me figured as the biggest fucking liar since Saddam Hussein!'

'And are you, girl, are you?'

'Ha?' Mandy gaped at him, the bear clutched now like a shield in front of her.

'Are you lying? Come on, kid, admit it: you got the whole

thing all rehearsed and off pat for Miss Lewis's recording. But the moment the PCA interviewer put on the pressure, what happened? Your story started to fall apart. Gaps, inconsistencies, holes opening up . . .'

'Hell, man, what is this? Whose side you on here?'

'The side of *truth*, Miss Trotter!' Suddenly the laid-back style was replaced by the hard-nosed criminal lawyer set on cracking a hostile witness. 'The side of integrity and justice! If you're lying here—if this statement's a load of bull—then believe me, kiddo, I've got to know it!'

There was a stunned silence, Mandy turning in shock to Bella who was scowling, her fists clenched in resentment. 'What is all this, man? What's with you here?'

'I don't make myself clear, Bella? Well now, let me spell it out for you both.'

He stood up to pace around as if in court; however, instead of enlarging his authority, the chintzy little room made him look somehow absurd. 'There is no way I'm getting egg on my face by floating a phoney witness. I get enough excrement from the Law Society and the rest of my legal brethren without being party to a case of aggravated perjury which could likely cost the state tens of thousands in retrial fees—not to say costing me whatever legal reputation I've managed to build up over the years.' He paused with a rhetorical flourish which all but toppled a china cat. 'That clear enough for you?'

Mandy was gasping, shaking her head, but Bella hugged a protective arm around her, hushing her to silence as she jabbed a finger at Randy. 'One thing you gotta know, Mr Bigshot, win or lose, true or false, the lawyer who fights the FAME side of this case won't never go short of clients— never again, you hear?' She nodded, still jabbing emphatically. 'You want to be Brixton's hero, you'll stop crowding this poor child here and you'll get on with the case.' She cocked her head in irony, adding a final jab at the man. 'Now, sir, is that clear enough for *you*?'

To which, acknowledging he'd met his rhetorical match, Randi inclined his head in a bow. 'Just one question for

you, Mama: how come you're wasting your sweet time in
the council chamber when you could be earning real bread
in the Old Bailey?'

The freckle-faced man sitting in the Range-Rover on the
far side of the street had the thin, wiry build of a jockey,
an impression enhanced by his Barbour coat and also the
cloth cap over his short-cropped gingery hair. Both the
ear-ring and the jewellery on his fingers, however, gave a
contrary impression, as did his habit of smoking cigars.

Terry Whittal's relaxed posture, fingers drumming in
time to the radio throb as he eyed the neat terrace house
into which Bella and Miss Lewis had gone with the tall
black geezer, gave little indication of the resentment seeth-
ing inside him. Sodding blacks: he'd never liked or trusted
them, not since way back when the Blades had dominated
the schoolyard at Hackney and that little black scrubber
had given him his first dose of the clap at the age of sixteen.
But too bad, there was no way a man of ambition could
really distance himself from them, not if his dealings were
illicit. Like it or not, their sheer black volume, be it in drugs,
blagging, tomming or what, made a measure of power shar-
ing as inevitable now as it had been way back in the days
of schoolyard overlording. One day, of course, just as soon
as he was far enough up the heap, things would change.
Landlords was about as high as nigs ever got. The *real*
rackets—the high-finance scams, the money-laundering
deals and all that—were nearly all white élitist. And that,
given a bit more time and power, was where Terry Whittal
was heading for sure.

Not like that plonker Alan Turnbull. He'd chosen the
underdog route in the service of Lystons, the huge multi-
national company Alan referred to as his 'corporate
employers'. Certainly, for all their hotels and travel agen-
cies, their City offices and stock-exchange listing, Lystons
plc were as greedy a mob of villains as you could wish to
find outside of the East End. Casinos and betting-shops
might take up only a relatively small number of pages at

the back end of the company's glossy annual report, but gambling was the powerhouse behind their huge opulence.

It was Alan's number at Lystons head office in the City that he dialled on his car-phone, explaining to the plummy-voiced secretary scrubber that it was a personal call from Terry and just to be a good girl and go tell the man.

'What's up, then?' Turnbull's tone was anything but welcoming. 'Come as quite a little surprise to have you calling me here.'

'Just a small favour, old mate. Nothing heavy. That country place you got down near Pangbourne. Empty just now, is it?'

'Why?'

'It looks like I might have this bit of special lined up, know what I mean? Need somewhere quiet and peaceful. Don't worry, we won't leave no mess: change the sheets and all that. Kosher, mate, you won't even know we was down there. OK with you, is it? Key in the usual place?'

'How long?'

'Ah, well now, my son, that depends on how long it takes me to, like, tickle her up. Soon, I'd say, the way things look. I'll bell you when we're through.'

Kate got Bella and Randi into the car and her key into the ignition before pretending to remember she'd left her scarf behind. 'Sorry. I won't be a minute.'

Fortunately, the scarf had not yet been noticed, so Kate was able to get back in to retrieve it from among the cuddlies as she remarked: 'Ari wasn't too happy about this evidence of yours. In fact he said he'd rather you dropped it.'

Mandy stared in surprise. 'You seen him?'

'We came straight here from the prison.'

'How—tell me, Miss Lewis, how does he look?'

'Just fine—most ebullient, er, jokey and high—until he heard about you.'

The young woman gestured, turning away as if to hide

guilt. 'Yeah, well, like I told you, he said all that before—years ago, when he said to forget what I seen and get out the country.' Then, swinging abruptly back in concern: 'He ain't changed none? No, how could you know that? Anyway, if he was laughing, he's got to be the same old Ari. Always fun, always the gent, always the daddy to me.'

It seemed odd to hear her talk with such obvious affection, given that the relationship between prostitute and pimp was traditionally more one of ruthless brutality than affection. Yet clearly, what Bella had told her about Ari's protecting and caring for his girls was true as far as this one was concerned.

'You really like him, huh?'

'Like him?' She giggled, fluttering her hands. 'Miss Lewis, he's the best thing ever happened to me. Before I met Ari, I was—well, I was just nothing, ha. Just an East Ham slag with no style nor class, know what I mean? The thought of me ever living in a place like this—Christ, I'd never dreamed it possible, ha.'

'So, er, naturally you're pretty keen to have him out of prison.'

It was almost embarrassing to ask such a loaded question, but the black girl merely nodded her head, bobbing around in artless enthusiasm. 'Damn sure! That bastard Mendoza what's been seeing after me since I come back from the Gulf, you wouldn't believe the shit he's been giving me! Hell, Miss Lewis, I'm going to have to go back to that old Arab daddy and his friends soon if things don't get better.'

'You mean, unless Ari gets out of prison soon?'

Mandy blinked, turning away in sudden guilt, only to give a shrill giggle as she saw Bella coming back along the street. 'Here's us two chattering on and Mama waiting out there.' She pushed Kate towards the door, still giggling shrilly. ''Bye, Miss Lewis. You and Mr Dubois be sure and get Ari out of there real soon like you said.'

Kate glanced in through the front window as she followed Bella back towards the car. Mandy had brought Ari-Bear

to wave goodbye, her pretty painted mouth open as she
laughed in childish expectation. Too bad, Kate reflected,
that she clearly hadn't a clue how turgidly the Law's delays
could bog things down. Even if they had some rock-solid,
irrevocable proof of Aristotle Edwards's innocence, as
opposed to the suspect testimony of such a late and biased
witness as Mandy Trotter, it could still take months before
his release.

As Kate drove off, waving to Mandy as they passed her
window, she did not of course notice the Range-Rover
parked on the further side of the street, its freckled owner
still apparently speaking into his car-phone.

Taff sighed, easing back on the accelerator for yet another
traffic tailback. Not a good day: first the visit from Barker
and then having to try and hype Thames Valley's worst-
ever crime figures. As usual, the Chief Constable had
cooked the figures so as to try and win increased resources
from the authority and extra manpower from the Home
Office. Needless to say, both bodies knew very well what
game he was playing. The chief constable was a fair leader
and an inspiration to the rank and file out there in the cars;
but by trying to play politics in his typically hammy way,
about all he'd achieve would be a lousy press, an alienated
police authority, and valuable ammunition for the single-
national-force lobby at Westminster.

It was even more of a relief than usual to get home at
last, change out of uniform and settle back into the trial
transcript midway through Ari's re-examination as his
counsel suavely sought to repair some of the damage
wrought by the Crown's cross-examination.

DEFENCE: Now, Mr Edwards, turning to this alleged confession which Detective-Inspector Barker claims you made
when first arrested—of which His Honour, in allowing the
jury to hear it, rightly reminded them that you strongly
deny the bulk.
AE: One thousand per cent denied, sir.

DEF: You deny actually saying any of the material after page two through to page ten, is that right?

AE: It is, sir.

DEF: And, as you said before, these signatures in your name at the foot of each page?

AE: Forged, every lousy one, sir.

DEF: And you stick to the account which you told to the jury during your evidence in chief of your movements just before, during and after the night of August the fifteenth last year?

AE: Every word of it true, sir. I was out drinking down the Mile End Road and never went nowhere near Arlene's place, not till the next afternoon.

DEF: Thank you. Now as to this so-called prison-yard confession of which the Crown has sought to make so much, you recall meeting Alfred Small in Brixton Prison?

AE: Like I said before, the little creep was in the same wing. Every day for a week or more he came and chatted me up—sat at the same table, asked me about this and that, offered no end of big deals once we was both outside again.

DEF: And he asked about your alleged offence?

AE: Sure, over and over. But hell, was I going to tell him lies or whatever just to impress him? No, sir, I told him the truth. I told him how I loved that girl Arlene and how there was no way I was going to let anyone harm her. No way. Nor was I going to harm her myself.

DEF: You heard Alfred Small give evidence to the jury.

AE: Sure. All that crap about her and this chick Janine—how I was beating the hell out of Arlene because of some lousy camera. I mean, no way did I say anything like he said. No way, sir. As for how come he could have known the name Janine McKane if it wasn't me told him, that's a question should be put to that pig Barker, not me.

Along with a lot of other questions, Taff thought, pausing from the transcript; like how come he's so desperate to head off any reopening of the case that he'll even drive down to

Thames Valley headquarters at Kidlington and threaten me!

'OK, sleuth,' he asked Kate once she'd arrived home and started to unwind, 'so what's the latest on Mandy Trotter?'

'Uh-uh, Taff.' She shook her head in curt rebuke. 'You stick to the trial transcript, OK.'

'Yeah, well, as it happens . . .'

'Nothing happens!' She pointed at the transcript. 'I was stupid even to have agreed to this.'

'If you'd just let me finish . . .'

'Taff, you promised, no involvement!'

'That's the whole point, love! Barker came and saw me. Today. Just out of the blue.' The lovely woman who was his destiny and the light of his life stood red-faced and swearing while he told her of the super's visit and his own obstinate attempts to fend him off. 'Of course he tried to swing the old copper's line, but then threw in a parting threat about the Leonard Snow case.'

'I'm off the story.' She headed abruptly for the kitchen, Taff hot on her heels.

'You what?'

'As of this moment, I'm finished with Bella and her whole stupid carnival.'

'Like hell you are!'

'Tomorrow morning, first thing, I'll be waiting at the news desk for Lawrence to arrive and—'

'Then Barker and Hammond will have won!'

'Like hell they will!' She gave a hard little laugh. 'Don't you worry, whoever Lawrence puts on to it—Desmond probably—will see it through to the death.'

'Except it's been yours for months now.' He tried to touch her but she bustled away to the fridge and then the dishes.

'So what? If they're threatening you, that's the end of it for me.'

'*Trying* to threaten, love. There's a world of difference.'

Kate paused, turning to meet his gaze at last. 'You were honestly one-hundred-per-cent solid on the Snow case?'

'Of course!'

It was not in fact true: Taff had planted forensic evidence and had cranked up a phoney witness. No matter that, at the eleventh hour they had been able to trip up Snow's wife in her evidence, unleashing a witness-box catharsis which had nailed the sly bastard more totally than any amount of forensic or corroborative evidence could ever have done. No matter that, once convicted, Snow had asked for 23 other indecent assaults on children to be taken into account. The fact remained that Taff had doctored some of the evidence and, with the unerring nose of a dog sniffing out a hot bitch, the Met lads had sussed him out. Whether they could ever expect to prove anything against him was highly unlikely. The prosecuting solicitor, now a regional CPS chief, was the one and only possible chink in Taff's armour and unlikely to wreck his own career by blabbing. Yet the weakness was there, the Met lads knew about it, had it on file somewhere and were capable of trotting it out whensoever they felt threatened by that cocky Welsh crusader Roberts.

'Listen to me, Kate, you don't want me trotting off to Lawrence Cawley to offer ITN my undercover services on the case.' She didn't bother with the denial, merely waved him a rude sign. 'OK then, just forget all about handing it over to Desmond Hammel.'

She scowled at him, then gave a reluctant shrug—only to go into renewed trauma when he asked her again what the latest was on Mandy Trotter.

'Why, for God's sake, Taff? *Why?* What the hell's it to do with you?'

'Simply that, if Barker's twitched up enough to come threatening me, it's on the cards he might try threatening her as well.'

She blinked in alarm, then shook her head. 'He wouldn't know where to find her.'

'Come on, this is the Met we're talking about. There's nothing they don't know about interfering with witnesses.'

Damn right, she thought, crossing to the telephone: if they can get a message into Wormwood Scrubs to put the frighteners on Ari Edwards, how much easier to track down Mandy's Bayswater hideaway!

There was no reply to the number. Kate let it ring a long time just in case Mandy was in the bath or, more likely, vacuuming around the massed ranks of cuddlies. Then she hung up and headed for the door. She tried to prevent her boy coming too but no chance.

There were lights on behind the curtains but no reply to their knocking. In fact, even while they waited on the step they heard the phone ring for a while inside.

'I'll try round the back. You stay here.'

In what seemed an amazingly short time, Taff was opening the front door to her. 'Come on in.'

'Did you force the back?'

'No need. It was unlocked.'

If Mandy had offered any resistance, the only signs of a possible struggle were in the front room where several of her precious Teds lay in disarray among the remains of a smashed China owl. Also they thought they could detect a lingering hint of chloroform.

Taff spent a long time checking for any possible forensic clues but could find nothing. In the bedroom there were signs of a suitcase having been hurriedly packed. Otherwise, nothing. Indeed, by the time they had finished searching around, even the chloroform smell had disappeared as totally as little Mandy Trotter.

CHAPTER 5

It was barely nine o'clock when they reached the FAME community centre but already the place was jumping to the reggae beat. How terrific, Kate thought, to find pretty Mandy here wearing chloroform-tinted perfume and wriggling her way through the sound barrier. But no such luck: there was no sign of her among the swaying throng of ethnic dancers or with Bella in the grandiose FAME office.

On the drive from Bayswater to Brixton, Kate had agreed there seemed little point in rushing off to report Mandy's disappearance. They had checked with her immediate neighbours, neither of whom had seen or heard anything of her departure; assuming she really had been snatched, it was unlikely her abductor would have risked leaving any prints around. 'And in any event,' she had pointed out, 'I'm damn sure the Met aren't going to send in an expensive forensics team to search for clues. Their attitude is bound to be that she's simply got cold feet about this statement she's made to the PCA—such cold feet she's decided to hop off to rejoin her Arab daddy in the Gulf'.

Bella seemed not in the least surprised to see them, the community centre being, after all, the mainspring of all natural life. However, her ebullience took an abrupt dive when Kate asked about Mandy.

'Of course she ain't here. That kid's going *nowhere*—not without one of us along with her. Purdah, that's how I told it to her. You stay put with your cats and your Teddies, I told her, stay right here until Miss Lewis and me tell you something else.'

She gave an abrupt groan, raising her clenched fists in the air, her eyes wide with alarm. 'So, Lord in Heaven, where *is* she?' Then, her eyes narrowing in anger, she exclaimed: 'Changed her mind, that's what! Lost her stomach for it. And you know who to blame for that? Mr Smart-Arse Lawyer, that's who! Coming on all tough with her like that at lunch-time.' She turned to Taff, her head into a series of rapid nods. 'He was cutting into her like she was some cheapo sham. Yelling at her about perjury and all. No wonder the poor kid's took off. No wonder!'

Kate started to tell her about the open backdoor, but Taff interrupted, instead edging her out as he told Bella to keep trying Mandy's number and also to put out the word among the black community in the hope of tracking her down.

As they emerged from the heat and throbbing rhythm

of the converted warehouse, Kate swung emphatically to confront her fiancé. 'OK, boyo, that's it. Finish. We go home to bed, and in the morning you go off to work as usual and forget you ever heard the name Mandy Trotter. Get it?'

Rather to her surprise, Taff bowed his head, nodding in suspiciously meek agreement.

'So Romeo checked around for clues while you talked to Mandy's neighbours before then leaving the place exactly as you'd found it, right?'

'Right.'

'Good.' The ITN editor sat back with a broad grin. 'Well done.'

'Lawrence, we just lost our one and only witness!'

'Lost a witness—who was about as believable as a builder's estimate—but gained a copper.'

'Huh?'

'Romeo Roberts.' He spread his hands in bland congratulations. 'Brilliantly done.'

'Listen, you devious bastard, will you just forget about Taff! He's family now, not—not dog's meat.'

The editor laughed at her, delighted with the way the story was building. Since they already had the tom witness recorded on video tape, her sudden disappearance tended to enhance rather than wreck the story. As for Kate's Welsh blade, time would show whether he could be both family *and* dog's meat. As for the accusation of being devious, since it came from one journalist to another, he took it as rather a compliment.

The disdain for Mandy Trotter's credibility was echoed by Foxy Walsh when Kate met him in the Bag o' Nails, the City pub round the corner from his security office.

'It merely seems to confirm what I said before about Mandy being Dame Bella's latest publicity gimmick.' He leered at her, bushy eyebrows thrust forward like a pair of snail's horns. 'Be honest now, did Bella show any *real* surprise about the kid's disappearance last night? Of course not. Because it's all part of her planned scenario.'

'Heaven's sake, Jack, even my editor didn't suss that possibility.'

'More than a possibility—highly probable.' He waved a thick file of press cuttings at her. 'I've been doing some homework on our Bella and there's a very regular pattern to her publicity stunts—namely, something big about every six months or so to boost the FAME fund-raising drives, and then a major do every time the council elections are getting near.' He raised his glass, his grin even broader. 'Guess what: Brixton's due to vote next month. Also she's been nominated as the party candidate to replace the Labour incumbent in Westminster.'

'So what are you saying? That Bella had been keeping Mandy up her sleeve all these years? That she finally gave her the witness script, schooled her in it, got me to get her on video tape and then along to the PCA, then paid her a wad to skip off back to the Gulf?'

He nodded, chuckling. 'Mama Media, eh.'

But was it, Kate wondered, really such a cynical bit of media manipulation? True, Bella's response to the news had seemed rather more theatrical than sincere. But, thinking about that afterwards, she'd wondered if Bella might have had a change of heart because of the violence to Ari in prison. If so, rather than have Mandy simply withdraw her PCA statement, she might have sought to keep the story alive, even heat it up, by spiriting the girl away.

'So the open backdoor, the chloroform and the signs of a struggle—you think they could all have been part of Bella's deception? To make it look like abduction?'

'With that woman, anything's possible.' Then, seemingly against his Bella theory, he asked: 'What about this lawyer bloke, Randi Dubois? Maybe he's moved her.' Then, at Kate's frown of confusion: 'If I had a hot witness like her, there's no way I'd want anyone knowing where she was— not even the TV people who were paying my fees.' He chuckled, winking as he drained his Scotch. 'Least of all the TV people.' He stood up, gesturing for her to follow. 'Enough chat, let's get some legwork done.'

'Such as?'

'I located Mandy Trotter's pimp, Angelo Mendoza. Come on.

PROS: In detail, please, Mr Small, as clearly as you can remember the conversation,

ALFRED JOHN SMALL: We'd been mates a couple of weeks when suddenly one evening, I remember we were sat together waiting to watch a movie in the rec . . .

PROS: That was the prison recreation hall?

AJS: Where they show the films, yes. Suddenly he says to me, Alfie mate, I want to tell you about what I done. I says no, because that is your secret, but he pleaded to tell it because he said he felt bad about it and he wanted to get it off his conscience. So then he said how he'd been running this Arlene Milton for a year or more, said what a terrific body she had and how he had the all-time hots for her despite, you know, managing her affairs for her. Any road, he said just because she had a terrific body didn't mean he could trust her. So one day in July he hid this automatic camera on a time switch in her room. And sure enough, he got some surprise pictures of a bird in there, some chick called Janine McKane who'd been hostessing with Arlene at Blandells Casino before she took up full-time with Ari.

PROS: The accused told you that he already knew this girl Janine McKane? That he recognized her in the pictures taken by his hidden camera?

AJS: That's right, yes. And he said how one picture showed Janine with a camera, so it was obvious what the pair of them was up to.

PROS: He said what exactly?

AJS: Said how they was going to take pictures of the customers, OK. Naturally Ari was very, very, very cut up about that. Much as he liked Arlene, there was no chance he could forgive her trying to pull a trick like that. And then, when he showed her the picture, he said she got really choked and angry back and called him a poxy nigger prat or some such and told him to stuff his pimping.

PROS: And what did he tell you then?

AJS: He was like half sobbing by then and he said he must have just freaked—blacked out, like—because the next thing he knew, she was lying there on the bed all smashed up.

PROS: Smashed up?

AJS: Finished, dead. So after that, he said there was nothing for it but just to sort of fold her into these big plastic bin-liners he'd got and get her outside to his car.

PROS: And then?

AJS: He said he just drove around till he found a building site, then carted the bag to where they'd dug out some footings ready for foundations, bunged it down the bottom and threw some earth in on top.

Taff looked up with a needless twinge of guilt as Sergeant Warboys knocked and came into the office.

'All OK, sir?'

'All what?'

'That schedule I did on the traffic statistics.'

'Ah.' He shifted the trial transcript aside, aware of the sergeant's curiosity over it. 'Give me a few minutes, Tony.'

'You've only got a couple before briefing time, sir.'

'Grief!'

'Of course if that lot—' he gestured towards the transcript—'if it's urgent, I could always . . .'

'No, no, nothing that can't wait.' It was an obvious cue to say what it was, but somehow, absurdly, Taff found himself sliding the heavy script into his briefcase. 'Just one I've been asked to review prior to appeal.' There was no reason on earth why he shouldn't have confided about it to his sergeant: this was Thames Valley turf, not London, moreover the mere fact that he wasn't fully prepared for the daily press briefing merited some explanation. But no, the instinct for caution born of years of involvement with the Met prevailed: he snapped the locks shut, stood

the briefcase in the corner by his coat and picked up the
briefing file. 'Let's go.'

It showed in Angelo Mendoza's face no less than his obese
figure that he was a man of gross appetites—the pouchiness
and sag, also a restless, rodent-like questing of the eyes.
Merely to see him scoffing an hors d'oeuvre in the furthest
corner of the Greek restaurant was to observe obsession
indulged.

'If Musha sent you here, Musha's got to watch his arse.
He owe you or something? You in finance or what?'

'Yes.' Jack Walsh reached out to take a bread stick. 'He
said you'd help us.'

'Not by feeding you,' the pimp growled, moving the
bread sticks to the further side of the table and crunching
one into his mouth. 'Help how?'

'One of your girls—Mandy Trotter . . .'

'Kid's on vacation. Too bad.' He smirked at Kate. 'Planning to have a screw show on TV, are you? Could be very
successful. There's a lot of punters just like to sit and look
at it. Be a lot of mileage in a show like that.' He started to
heave and shake, tickled at the prospect.

'What do you mean—vacation?' Walsh asked, waving
an expectant waiter away from the table. 'How long?'

'Too long!' Mendoza belched, flicking crumbs irritably
from the front of his brocaded waistcoat. 'She's been bloody
weeks away.'

'Been with Bella Edwards, right?'

The pouchy, porcine eyes swivelled towards Kate. 'You
know so much, you know more than me. Only thing I
can tell you, I'm losing customers. Lazy slag, that's what.
Unreliable. Typical black.' He sucked down an oyster. 'So
what else you can tell me? What's this about Bella? This
all got something to do with that prat husband of hers?'

'You know Mandy used to be with him?'

'Of course I know.' He beckoned the waiter back again
to demand more asparagus before resuming to Kate. 'Ari
spoilt the slag rotten. It cost me a lot of hard work to knock

her into shape.' He paused to peer closely at Walsh. 'What is it with you, fella? You've got a mean face, you know that? You should eat more, flesh yourself out. I seen punters like you: mean and hungry. You a cop or what? No, don't answer that. If Musha's sleeping with cops, he's even worse than what I thought.'

'If I was a cop, I wouldn't be with the media.'

'No? Why not? Everyone sells out to the Box these days. The great god, that's what. You heard what happened to this English punter what went to a cat-house in Paris? After he'd had his bit of tail, the Madam tells him the price is two hundred francs. Two hundred, he yells, so how come you only charged my friend one hundred last night? Because, Monsieur, the Madam tells him, tonight we ain't on television.' He reverted to chuckles and shakes and belches, beckoning yet again to the waiter.

'The way I heard it,' Kate remarked, 'Ari Edwards managed all his girls in the same easy-going way.'

'More fool him!' Munch-munch. 'Look what it cost him in the end, huh! That slag of his, Arlene whatsit, taking diabolical liberties. She wouldn't have had the cheek to do a stupid thing like that—not if he'd treated her right and kept her in line. Instead he caught her at it—caught her trying to cheat—and had to teach her a lesson.' The sagging bulk heaved in a shrug. 'Too bad he happened to go too far. Typical black, see. No finesse.'

He gestured for the waiter to pour him more wine. 'But the way he treated la Trotter was even worse. You wouldn't believe the mess he left her in.'

'Mess?'

'Heart-struck,' he sneered, miming the playing of a gipsy fiddle with his knife and fork. 'Can you imagine that? She's working her fanny off for the big ape and figures she's in love with him at the same time.' He paused to dip a prawn into sauce and pop it into his already full mouth, meanwhile leering at Kate. 'That's love for you, Ms Lewis. L-O-V-E.'

If so, Kate thought, maybe she took off from the Bayswater flat of her own volition, not wanting to foul up with her beloved Ari.

'She's just disappeared,' she told the guzzling pimp. 'Have you any idea where she might have gone?'

'Why ask me? I'm just her manager. How I should know?' He went into a mild choking fit, eyeing Walsh and Kate as he gulped down wine to subdue it. 'You think I should care? Look, I got a full stable. Her I can do without. I don't depend on no dumb-brain black slag. More trouble than she was worth. Good riddance.'

'So you've no clue where she might have gone—such as to a relative, perhaps?'

'I ain't into welfare, Ms Lewis.' He mopped his brow with his napkin then leered at her again. 'Only the welfare of the punters, huh, helping them with their problem. That's enough good works for one man.'

The community centre's office was large and furnished with enough sofas and easy chairs to seat a full meeting of the FAME team. The walls were decorated with the posters and placards of past campaigns—also with press pictures of the team's more spectacular stunts, such as bungee-roping off Holborn Viaduct, bikinied abseiling down St Paul's during the Lord Mayor's Show, and acrobatic stunts at both Wimbledon and Wembley.

The two main stalwarts, Leena and Winston, had been with Bella since Ari's murder trial. Since both were professional dancers, it followed they had attracted athletic youngsters with a flair for dancing who also happened to be unemployed, daring, highly-strung show-offs. Hence the babble of wisecracks and pantomime, laughter and cartwheels which characterized FAME meetings.

Man, what if we hit the Palace? Or Westminster? Or, hey, what if we hit them both together? What if, what if, what if? We might be able to use this wacky kid I met who models in Claridge's. What if we got the mini-cab drivers giving out leaflets? Man, you wait till they hear my new

Ari number: FAME sure is a-coming to Radio One. What if, what if, what if?

They had already asked Bella about the progress of this Mandy Trotter thing and had been puzzled by the flatness of her response. They had anyway been puzzled by the need for a planning meeting at all, having not long heard that Mandy's evidence was exactly the magic they needed to force a retrial. If it was really the best news in six years of the *Free Aristotle Macho Edwards* campaign, what was coming down here, man?

They had been at it for little more than a couple of drinks' worth and were barely starting to get the ideas popping, when the phone rang on the big executive desk.

'Hello, this here's FAME Land, who calls?'

'Bella there?' The man's tone was tense and menacing.

'Sure thing.' Leena held the phone across. 'Sounds like a cop.'

'Yeah?' She took the phone, waving for silence. 'Councillor Edwards speaking. Who's this?'

'Get rid of the company. I want a word in your ear.'

'Hold on.' She pressed the S-button and told the team not to make a sound before resuming into the phone. 'So who is this?'

'You know damn well. Now just pay attention because I'm saying this only once. Forget Mandy Trotter. She's history now. Just a bad dream. Same way Ari's going to be if you don't pack in your sodding crusade. I know it suits you very well, *Councillor*. All that publicity. But enough's enough, OK? I sent him one message already—ignored. So the one I sent him today is definitely a final warning. Next time they won't just put in the boot; next time he's for the drop. No question about it. You pack it in or he's dead.'

The phone clicked as he rang off. Bella sat scowling heavily at it, then placed it slowly back on the receiver before looking up at the circle of expectant black faces.

'Leena, honey,' she said at last, 'be an angel and get me the number of Wormwood Scrubs prison.'

Kate leaned over to open the Polo's passenger door as Bella lumbered across from the tube station, then eased her bum down into the front seat.

'When you called, I hoped maybe you'd had some news about Mandy.' However, when Bella merely shook her head, she added: 'No. Well, hoped rather than expected.'

The black woman stared bleakly at her, then slowly shook her head. 'You got bad vibes going, too, huh. Honey, let me tell you, after you and your fancy man came looking for her last night, I really got to worrying about that kid.' She checked as a sob of abrupt remorse tightened her throat. 'And whose fault, huh! Lord, if only I'd had the plain common decency to stop her—just to tell her, no, Mandy baby, this ain't no good, not any more, not six years later. Do as Ari told you; that's what I should have told her. But no, damn it, I had to go and shout Alleluia and call you in on it and start the whole great roller-coaster on the move! And now—now . . . oh, that poor innocent kiddie!'

Kate gave her a hug, finding a tissue as tears welled in the woman's eyes, wondering at the rush of emotion. Finally she started the car and moved off towards the underpass. 'The prison, right?'

'Right,' Bella snuffled miserably. 'And this here's my fault and all!'

'Er, what here, Bella?'

'My poor darling Ari.'

They were escorted by one of the gate officers along to the prison hospital which was housed in a separate building between the old prison wall and the inner electrified security fence. Kate, never one to miss an opportunity, tried her best to chat up the guard, but he maintained an embarrassed silence, speaking only when Bella accused him of callous indifference.

'It's not that we don't care, madam,' he muttered, scarlet-faced. 'On the contrary, many of us take the task very much to heart. More than is good for us, given the workload.'

Bella was making cooing noises in mock sympathy, but Kate cut her off. 'OK, so you're all frustrated social workers trying to do a job which, because the Home Office insists on such stingy manning levels, forces you to be overworked turnkeys. So what's new? Why does that have to prevent you saying anything about what's happened to Ari Edwards?'

The officer paused, his key in the hospital entrance door. 'Because you happen to be media, Miss Lewis.' He thrust the door open for them as he added: 'Which, I regret to say, means I daren't trust you.'

And *touché* for you, Kate old girl, she thought, giving him a wink as she followed Bella inside to where the nursing orderly was waiting to lead them upstairs and along the corridor.

Amazingly, although heavily strapped up, Ari managed to give Bella a wry twinkle from the depths of his bandages, meanwhile beckoning her close for a kiss. 'Look at her! Come to cheer me up and all she can do is stand there blubbing like a little girl.'

'Sorry, Daddy, sorry. It just breaks me up to see you pained like this.'

'No, sweetie-pie,' he grinned, 'pain comes when the dope wears off.' He registered Kate's presence, his bruised face tightening in concern. 'Say, Miss Lewis, what the heck?'

'Hello, Ari.'

'I didn't even want Bella to know, but as for the TV . . .'

'No problem,' she told him. 'So long as no one leaks it to the Beeb, you can relax.'

He nodded in solemn acceptance of her word, then eyed his wife. 'So who leaked it to you, honey? I told them screws, listen, you don't go fretting my sweet lady with all this shit.' He sighed, rolling his one functional eye. 'They promised me.'

''Cepting maybe they had no choice.' Bella shrugged, avoiding any mention of the telephoned ultimatum she'd had from Terry Whittal. 'Maybe they figured they had to notify next of kin.'

'Ain't no way they thought I was going under!' Ari exclaimed with a hollow chuckle. 'This here Holiday Inn specializes in knuckle-sandwich breakfasts.'

He stated it as a fact, with no trace of false heroism. Yet, for all the effect of the painkillers, there was no doubting the grievous extent of his injuries: a bed-cage over his legs, an arm in plaster, his chest and head heavily bandaged.

'That big-mouth lawyer said he'd get you safe into solitary. Gave me his solemn promise.'

'Why?' the black man asked her quietly. 'Was that your compromise? Get me locked away in the block so you can keep your Mandy witness up and going?' There was a pause, his wife scowling and evasive. 'Don't nobody listen to the word from in here no more? Don't your Ari have no say in his own freaking future?'

'Don't talk that way, baby!'

'I told you . . .' he had to pause, gasping for breath, bloodstained spittle dribbling from his mouth. 'That girl says nothing.'

'She ain't,' the woman retorted over-quickly. 'Not one word.'

'How, honey, how can I believe you?' His eyes swung balefully to Kate. 'That the truth?'

''Course it is!' Bella snapped.

'Miss Lewis?'

'Presumably.' Kate shrugged, damned if she was going to play Bella's devious games. 'Since she's disappeared.'

The effect was galvanic, the injured man staring appalled as Kate explained the circumstances which made it look as if Mandy had been abducted, then finally lying motionless, his eyes closed and only the pulsing veins in his neck to convey the depth of his anguish. Bella tried to play it down, insisting the girl had merely run off of her own accord, but her husband waved her to silence.

'Miss Lewis,' he muttered at last through gritted teeth, his voice hoarse with determination, 'six years I done in this place, plus one on remand. All the stunts my wife and the FAME team been at to get me a retrial was all on their own accord. Maybe that's 'cos they hold me innocent, maybe they got other reasons of their own.' He paused, swatting with his unplastered arm to silence his wife's protests. 'Whichever, Bella, whichever way it is, you ain't never consulted me. Why? 'Cos you knew if you had done I'd have said to leave it lie.'

'Ari babe, on my life—'

'No, woman, no more, no more. The time for all that's done and gone now.' His good eye swivelled to fix on Kate. 'Miss Lewis, from this moment, Ari Edwards wants out of this place. You understand me? *Out*. Nothing hidden, the full story exclusive to ITN—free—just so long as I get outside of these walls!'

CHAPTER 6

'In emotion veritas, eh?' Jack Walsh sat back at his desk and gave Kate his sardonic grin.

However, she thought, perhaps the shell of cynicism formed over his years of CID work did have some virtues. It was a cynicism from which she herself was by no means immune, except that the seen-it-all response of the journalist tended to be less personal. With coppers, the lies and deceit, the sham and counterfeit, all represented a direct challenge to their professionalism: it was a vital part of their job to sift truth from lies, suss out the facts from the web of deception. Since they were called so often to deal with society's grubbier, less capable elements, it was only human of them to end up taking a fairly sceptical view of things. It was, for CID in particular, an occupational hazard— and probably added to the high-risk status of the average copper's marriage.

The ITN crime reporter, however, while prey to similar pressures, needed to retain at least a show of credence if only to avoid offending Joe Public. Kate may indeed over the years have seen it all, but perhaps more objectively than the officers whose hazardous job it was to deal with crime.

'Maybe,' she shrugged, 'maybe the pain-killers were acting a bit like a truth drug. Whatever the explanation, I just felt—very strongly—that he was sincere. More than that, for the first time, I really got the feeling he is innocent and bloody well shouldn't be locked away in the Scrubs.'

She sat back, cocking her head at him, only to guffaw at his expression. 'I know, I know, it sounds corny put like that. But really, up until now, I haven't much cared whether he was guilty or not because the driving force has been the story: all Bella's tricks and gimmicks, then on top of all that, sex-pot Mandy with her extraordinary evidence. Terrific stuff, to quote my nauseating editor. I honestly haven't much cared whether it was true or not—perhaps, at heart, because I haven't felt able to believe very much of it.'

'Whereas now,' the ex-copper drawled in irony, 'they finally hooked you.'

'Don't you see, they didn't *need* to. I was going with it regardless. And no one knew that better than Bella. Damn it, you're the one who pointed out how inspired she is at manipulating the press.'

'I also pointed out that Ari Edwards is guilty as hell, no question.'

'Well, I just wish you could have been there to see him. He was lying back all smashed up and heavily doped and telling me—*me*, not Bella—that suddenly, for the first time, he wanted out.'

Walsh cleared his throat, leaning across to pour Kate more coffee. 'Which sounds to me far more like vengeance than innocence.' Then, persisting over Kate's objections: 'We heard from Angelo Mendoza how sweet Mandy is on Ari. Maybe it's mutual. That way, the moment he hears from you that she's disappeared, boom-boom, suddenly he wants out!'

'Except . . .'

'What?'

She shrugged. 'I know it sounds like your typical naïve

hunch, but I did get the very strong feeling this was the moment of truth for him. For whatever reason, presumably fear, he's been resigned to serving his time. And now, as you said, possibly out of vengeance, all that has changed and he wants out. But the point is, he knows we can clear him and get him out because he knows he's genuinely innocent.'

'Ah!'

'Otherwise,' she persisted, ignoring his CID snort, 'otherwise, we wouldn't stand a chance in hell of reversing the murder conviction.'

Walsh unwrapped a stick of gum, clamping his teeth into it with all the compulsion of a smoker lighting up a fag. 'Fear,' he conceded at last, 'you reckon he's been sweating out his sentence through fear. So presumably what you're saying is that he didn't kill Arlene Milton, but he knows who did.'

It was while sitting in the usual traffic snarl-up along Marylebone that Kate got the call from the ITN Newsroom. 'A woman asking for you, Miss Lewis. Identified herself as Mandy Trotter and would you call her on 0831 222350.'

Kate managed to pull across into a side-street but dialled the number in vain. In the event, her first three tries proved fruitless—nothing new, particularly with one car phone trying to call another. It was only after she moved the car along and tried yet again that she finally got through, the call answered by a woman who was panting and breathless and definitely not Mandy.

'Hello, yes?'

'Is Mandy Trotter there, please?'

'That's Miss Lewis, right? Mandy was waiting for you to call. She wants you to meet her.'

'What?' Kate's initial surge of relief took a dip. 'Isn't she there now?'

'She waited long as she could, Miss Lewis. She wants you to meet her near St Katherine's yacht basin. Said for you to go to East Smithfield and she'll meet you in Cable

Lane down the far end of Thomas More Street. Got that?'

'No.' Then, cutting in when the woman started to repeat the instructions: 'I mean, no I'm not going to docklands at this time of the evening without at least hearing it directly from Mandy herself.'

'Suit yourself, miss. But she was desperate for you to be there, I'll tell you that. Desperate. Waited long as she could, then begged me to hang on here for when you rang.'

Kate started to ask who she was and where she was speaking from, but the woman merely repeated the rendez-vous, her voice increasingly urgent before hanging up. Kate dialled the number in vain a couple more times, then tried to ring Jack Walsh. No luck: his office number merely gave her an Ansaphone, his car-phone number gave engaged.

She pulled out the street map and turned to the Tower Bridge area. Thomas More Street looked distinctly remote, winding down to where, just short of the river, Cable Lane led into a dead-end. She tried Walsh again, then swore angrily.

It was by no means a new dilemma for Kate. She well knew what answer to expect if she rang her male-chauvinist editor, likewise what her ever-protective Taff would say. They, in fact, were the two main reasons she had got herself set up with old Foxy Walsh—as minder as much as sleuth. But now, as with all the best laid plans . . .

Wheel along there anyway, she decided. Since Jack worked from the City and lived east-side, he was likely to be not too far from the docks whenever she did manage to make contact. Meanwhile, she would hardly be risking her all by at least driving to the vicinity of the rendezvous.

The fine line between courageous resolve and idiot reck-lessness was never too clear for Kate Lewis. Whereas she was amply capable of fear, the simple avoidance of danger was woefully less clear cut than for those in more normal jobs. More than the job, however, she seemed compelled to venture far further into threat than the majority of her crime-reporter colleagues. It was a compulsion which ran way back to the depths of her troubled childhood. For, just as she had to keep forcing herself to subdue her shyness every time she was due to go before the cameras, so she had to keep proving she had not one whit less grit than the boy her father had so emphatically wanted her to be.

After the traffic congesting Cornhill, Leadenhall Street and Aldgate, she found Minories suddenly clear and East Smithfield all but empty. Although Thomas More Street still had a few commercial vehicles parked outside the various workshops and warehouses along its earlier section, its straight far end was largely deserted. But not entirely. Parked just beyond the entrance to Cable Lane was a grubby Range-Rover.

The body had been buried in a shallow grave in National Trust woodland near Marlbury. It was found by a mongrel whose owner thought the dog was digging for rabbits until he saw the skin and torn flesh of the woman's foot.

It was mid-afternoon before Taff had arrived, by which time the area was already cordoned off and uniformed officers had commenced an initial search of the area under the supervision of a local sergeant. Also by then, to the chagrin of the young CID inspector provisionally in charge of the investigation, members of the press corps were starting to arrive.

'The main thing is to avoid giving them the old no-comment routine,' Taff told the Investigating Officer. 'I suggest you give them a quickie interview now; then we'll find them facilities locally, get them all set up with phones and so on, and promise them a full press conference this evening in good time for the dailies to catch their deadlines.'

'Why don't we give them a full guided tour,' the inspector muttered. 'They might find us some clues.'

Taff grinned in sympathy with the man's frustration. 'We'll do that tomorrow morning, Rob. We'll find a badgers' sett well away from the actual scene and lay out false tapes for them, then they can trample around and take as many pictures as they like without destroying anything.'

The prospect of such a trick finally drew a thin smile

from the inspector. 'So how much do I tell them now?'

'Time and circumstances of discovery. Any preliminaries you can on the victim such as approximate age, skin and hair colour, type of injuries, clothed or naked, prospects of identification. Tell them how soon you expect the remains to be moved and where. Also the names of the best pubs around here.'

The CID man nodded, busy with his notebook. 'Did Kidlington say anything about who'll be running the show?'

'Not yet. Do this well, Rob, and they'll be in even less of a rush.'

'Damn it, guv'nor, a murder!'

'There's got to be a first for everyone.' He gestured to where the press people were gathered near the police cars beside the road. 'All set?'

'What shall I say about the facilities?'

'That I'm laying it on soon as I can find somewhere. The village hall down the road looked promising—assuming they haven't got a barn dance booked for tonight. All set?'

It had gone off reasonably well, the inspector managing to conceal his resentment during the initial briefing, the hall proving not only available but suitable for communications hook-ups. Well before the evening briefing, a superintendent arrived from HQ to oversee things, enabling Taff to get away earlier than expected.

There was no sign of Kate when he got home, nor any message from her on the Ansaphone. He dialled the ITN newsroom and was surprised to hear she'd left well over an hour earlier, apparently heading for home.

'Hello, Jack, reached you at last.'

'What can I do for you, girl?' He listened to the car-phone in rising alarm, noting the rendezvous point, then told her to lock herself into the car and drive back up to the junction with East Smithfield.

She never got the chance. As she leaned across to lock the passenger door, the first of several hammer blows smashed into the driver's window. Kate reached desperately for the ignition, glass fragments raining in as her hand found the key. She turned it, gunning the engine. But even as she tried to ram into gear, a hand forced in to switch off and snatch the key.

'Out, you bitch, out!' Kate writhed across to the further side, but he had the driver's door unlocked and open before she could get half way. 'Out, I said!'

He still held the masonry hammer he'd used to smash the window, brandishing it in her face as he dragged her violently back across and out of the car.

Despite the surge of blind panic which gripped her limbs more tightly even than the man's grasp, Kate found a part of her mind somehow standing aside in a detached, almost clinical way, as if to observe the assault—weighing progress, watchful for retaliation, assessing the man's intentions.

Not that she could see much of him as yet. The darkness apart, he had doubled her arms round behind her back so that she hung forward, head down like a rag doll. Don't resist, she kept telling herself, hang limp so he thinks you're acquiescent or even unconscious. That way, he might just get cocky enough for you to get one real go at him: one chop, one kungfu kick, just one . . .

'A message for you,' the man grunted, half carrying and half dragging her along the lane, then down an alleyway before at last letting her slump to the ground as he crouched beside her. 'Think you're so high and mighty, don't yer. The bigshot celebrity!'

At last he released her arms and heaved her over on to her back. She kept her eyes rolled upwards, feigning unconsciousness, forcing herself to remain inert as she felt his hands ripping the clothing off her body.

'The message, Miss Bigshot, is the same as was sent that black arsehole in the nick!' She flinched involuntarily as she felt him groping at her breasts and then tearing off her underwear and gripping her vagina. Lie back, stay limp; he's got to get vulnerable eventually. And then . . .

He was hurting her now, his grip savage and intense as

his excitement rose, a dark shape grunting and slavering over her like a rutting boar. Don't yell out, not yet! Wait, wait, wait! Let him get erect, get the blood down there, get him vulnerable . . .

In the event, she timed it to perfection, her knee flying up like a piston to whack into his tackle with such desperate force it lifted him up and half across her. Instantly she was wriggling to get free, barely aware of his agonized yell. She was almost out from his writhing form, was trying to roll clear, when his hand clamped on her wrist. She swung back, lunging to bite him. Then, hard under her back, she felt the big hammer. She snatched wildly for it with her free hand, raising and swinging it in a frenzy, again and again, raining blows until finally the grip slackened on her wrist.

At last she was able to roll free, heaving to her knees, then clawing her way up the nearby wall to reel away along the alley. She staggered the twenty or so metres back along the lane, saw the Polo across the far side of the street and stumbled desperately towards its open door.

The keys had gone. Briefly she gave way to despair, slumping over the wheel with a strangled cry. But then, gritting her teeth, she forced herself to start searching. As she did so, headlights flooded on from a vehicle parked further along on the opposite side. On the impulse, Kate got up and, waving her arms, started across. As she did so, the engine roared to life, gears grated and the vehicle leapt forward, swinging fast towards her.

She gasped, lurching instinctively aside. The lights swung after her, fast and remorseless; but, although the wing struck her, it was only a glancing blow, thumping her in the flank and pitching her flat on the tarmac. Sobbing in terror, she struggled up again in time to see the Range-Rover's reversing light come on as the unseen driver slammed into reverse to hurtle backwards at her. Dazed with shock, she again flung herself aside, only to whack heavily up against a traffic sign. In the event, it was the sign which saved her, taking the main impact of the rear bumper as Kate fell half under the back. Briefly the engine raced, tyres spinning fiercely beside her. Then the driver leapt out and darted back to her.

He had actually reached her, was in the act of grabbing her hair when headlights flashed across his face and a car hooted. The man swore in fury and raced back to leap into the front. Instantly the engine revved and the vehicle shot forward, swerving wildly past the oncoming car and away towards East Smithfield.

Heart pounding wildly, Kate huddled down to hide her nakedness, praying to God it was Foxy Walsh and not some marauding opportunist.

'Bloody hellfire!' The voice sounded like his, but even so she wasn't fully sure until he'd rushed across to crouch beside her. 'Dear God, Kate!'

Sobs burst from her as he picked her up, carrying her like a child to his car.

He wanted to drive her straight to the nearest hospital, but she managed to stop him. Instead, giving way at last to shock, she slumped in the front seat, shuddering and whimpering while Walsh muttered in reassurance, then wrapped his jacket around her shoulders and hugged her close.

He left it several minutes before urging her to try and talk. Even so, it took another minute or so before she was able to subdue the horror sufficiently to try and speak. And then, just as she was stammering out about the alleyway down the lane, she saw the hunched dark figure come tottering out of it. Involuntarily, she screamed, pointing as she gasped for Walsh to get him, get him, get him!

It was easy enough. The rapist was still dazed and groggy from the hammer blows to his head and body, much less the kneeing of his testicles. He offered no resistance as Walsh frog-marched him across and heaved him into the rear of the car.

'Right, then,' the detective muttered, easing in after him then leaning forward once again to reassure Kate. 'He won't hurt you any more, girlie, don't worry. Don't be afraid.'

They sat for a while longer, Kate still fighting to subdue her sobs and the awful trembling which had seized her body, the man groaning and holding his head as he muttered for a hospital.

Finally Walsh took hold of his shoulders, heaving him round so he could glare into his face. 'I'm a retired police chief superintendent,' he snapped, 'and I'm arresting you for assaulting this lady. Before I do so, however, I'm going to give you the opportunity to come clean and tell me exactly what happened.'

PROS: Mr Edwards, the custody sheet, signed by you in the presence of the custody officer, Sergeant Harlow, and the investigating officer, DCI Barker, clearly states that, after being read your rights, you specifically rejected the offer of having a lawyer present at your interrogation.

AE: Lies, sir.

PROS: Whose lies, Mr Edwards? Your lies?

AE: I never signed nothing to say I wanted no lawyer. Never.

PROS: Look again at your copy of the custody sheet. You deny that is your signature at the foot of the document? Before you answer that, bear in mind it would be possible for the court to have that signature examined by handwriting experts to compare its authenticity against other samples of your signature.

AE: See here, sir, if that is mine, it's because I didn't understand what I was signing there.

PROS: You didn't understand? Are you telling the jury you're illiterate?

AE: They take your money, your keys and stuff, take everything except the clothes off your back. They take it all at the same time as they fill out that form. The pigs had been leaning on me real heavy all the way to the station. By then, I didn't know my butt from my honky. Next thing they're telling me to sign here and there and here. OK, so I signed. I sure as hell wasn't signing to say I didn't want no lawyer. About the only damn thing I had been saying ever since they picked me up was how I wanted a lawyer. I ain't saying nothing without a lawyer, that's what I kept telling them. Nothing without a lawyer. Nothing, nothing, nothing. So, believe me, sir, there was no way I was going to go signing how I didn't want one. No chance.

PROS: Mr Edwards, you heard Sergeant Harlow and DCI Barker both give evidence during the prosecution case of how the custody officer specifically drew your attention to your right to have a lawyer present.

AE: Sure I heard them say that, sir, and they was both lying in their teeth.

Taff dumped the transcript down, snatched up the phone yet again and dialled Jack Walsh's home number. It rang only briefly before being answered by his wife.

'Hello, Dell, Taff Roberts here. You got Jack at home there?'

'I haven't, Taff. I was hoping it might be him calling.'

'Do you happen to know where he is by any chance?'

'Wish I did, sorry.'

'It's important.' He and Dell Walsh went back ten years or more to when Taff had first joined the Yard's serious fraud team under her husband. Old Jack, doting father that he was, had promptly tried to pair off the bushy-tailed Welsh detective-sergeant with his daughter Heather, contriving various excuses to get him along to the Walsh household.

For her part, Dell had weighed Taff up at the far more prosaic level of whether he was likely to boost or curtail her husband's drink habit. Having decided the sergeant seemed a responsible sort of lad more likely to keep Jack in line than lead him astray, she had done all she could to boost him up with her erratic husband, while at the same time discouraging Jack's hopes of romance. After all, no one knew better than Dell what a bloody awful deal coppers' wives had to put up with, so why wish it on her only daughter!

'He rang me about sixish to say he'd just left the office

and was going for a beer on the way home. Then, just short of seven, he rang me again, sounded a bit tense he did, said something urgent had come up and he'd ring me soon as ever.'

Nearly a bloody hour ago, Taff thought. 'You've no idea what it's to do with?'

'I was going to ask you the same thing, Taff.' She gave an embarrassed little grunt. 'Silly thing, eh. Three or four years now since he left the force—I'd forgotten what it's like—the worry, you know. The grass widow, sitting at home fretting. Of course, you wouldn't know, always out there among the action.'

'Ha. I'm beginning to find out, Dell, believe me.'

'What, with your Katie, you mean? Rather puts us both in the same boat tonight, don't it.' She checked at the indiscretion, then added: 'Well, you must know she's got Jack doing some work for ITN, so I'm not speaking out of turn. Consultancy, that's what it's supposed to be. But I'll bet he's out there gumshoeing around like a DC on his first stake-out. Big idiot. You'd think he'd grow up, wouldn't you. I mean, it's not as if we need the money. Had pots of cash ever since he joined Klein's. No, it's the excitement, that's what he misses. The chase. You lot, you're all the same: behind the uniforms and the rule-books, you're all blessed Wyatt Earps.'

She paused at last, repeating the embarrassed grunt. 'There I go, letting off at you like old times, eh, Taff. It's good to have a talk again, though. Come and see us soon, won't you.' She paused again. 'When you hear anything, let me know. I'll do the same if I hear first. Cheerio, son. Take care.'

Taff rang off and promptly dialled through to check the ITN newsroom again. Still no news of her. And a big welcome to Taff Roberts, he thought as he rang off, hello to the Grass Widows Club.

'It was this tom I know called Maureen—she's the one

what put me up to it. Bunged me a couple of hundred, she did, and told me where to be and when.'

Kate couldn't bring herself to look at the evil swine. She merely sat listening as Jack Walsh interrogated him in the back of the car, sat hunched in shock and loathing, one part of her wanting to blot it out, the other hypnotized by what he was saying.

His tone was whining and self-pitying, a long way indeed from the brutish threats and violence of earlier. So far that, were it not for his injuries—the gory hammer blows to his head and acutely bruised testicles—she could even have believed they had the wrong man. But what was new about that? Put the brutal mugger in the dock with a hair-cut, a clean white shirt and a sympathetic probation report, and the bench would be hard put to see him as such a terrifying monster.

'Maureen who?' Walsh's voice was unnaturally soft. 'Where can we find her?'

'Search me, mate. Just seen her around. Far as I know, her beat's around Paddington somewhere. All I can tell you, she come up to me in the Jolly Jack, that's my usual pub, told me where and when and said to get on and do the business. Do a good job, she said, and you'll be in for a freebie next time we meet.'

'You've done this sort of, er, business for her before?'

'Not Maureen, like, but I've done a favour for one or two agents—well, pimps and that. Just to help 'em out, like.'

What a wonderful trade, Kate thought. And just how does he fill in the job-description box on the DSS form? Sex Aid? Screw Artist? Rent-a-Rape?

She had managed to control the trembling now and hold back the sobs. But in the wake of the hysteria had come pain: the sting of the numerous skin abrasions and the ache of all the bruises along with the onset of a migraine. Earlier, Walsh had secured the man's wrists with his trouser belt, then reversed down Cable Lane to the mouth of the alley-way. Then, using a torch, he had gone and retrieved Kate's soiled clothing and shoes along with the masonry hammer and her car keys.

'So Maureen told you where to be and when.'

'Right. I was waiting here for hours.'

'In the car with the other bloke?'

'What car? No such luck. I was stood across there shivering in the bloody cold. Enough to turn you off, mate, I tell yer.'

'Too bad it didn't do just that, *mate*. It would have saved you a whole lot of trouble.'

'Yeah, well, as to that,' the rapist retorted with a groan, 'how much longer before you get me to a doctor? Wouldn't be surprised if that bitch ain't cracked me skull, not to mention a couple of ruptured pillocks.'

'You'll get to a doc just as soon as you've told us the goods.' The ex-copper's voice was silky soft, like a stripper peeling away the layers of lies and deceit until he gets to the naked truth beneath; the product of all those years of CID experience, Kate thought, the bulk of it well pre-PACE when the interrogation process was still a largely covert ritual, usually played out with a partner, Mr Soft and Mr Hard, unhindered by the need for tape-recordings or vigilant lawyers.

'So this Maureen told you where and when. What about who?'

'She gave me the number of this red Polo and a photo—well, a press-cutting, it was.'

'So you knew exactly who it was you were coming after.'

'Sure.' He snorted. 'Made all the difference, didn't it. All them times I'd seen madam's mug up there on the screen and thought to meself, Gawd, I couldn't half give you one! Then suddenly here's Maureen bunging me a coupla of ton to come and do what I'd have done for nothing!'

Kate was shuddering again, oppressed by the man's lurid reply. It was nothing new, of course. On the contrary, the dread of all those freaks and perverts out there among the watching millions, weaving their kinky plans and fantasies was always there. It was something she and her women

colleagues exchanged sick jokes about in a lame attempt to
ward off the demons. But now to hear it articulated like
this was appalling.

'What about the message?' she snapped, finding her voice
at last. 'The same as was sent to the black arsehole in
prison, that's what you said.'

There was a startled pause with only the sound of heavy
breathing from behind her in the back of the car.

'Go on,' Walsh prompted at last, 'answer the lady. What
about the message?'

'Nothing to add,' the man whined. 'Maureen just said to
be sure and pass on the message. Said to tell you to pack
in the whole Edwards story or you're for the drop like him.'
He guffawed. 'Old slag said I was to be sure and ram home
the message.'

Kate winced in renewed revulsion at the proximity to
evil—to have come within an ace of rape itself and now to
gain this insight into the brutish mentality.

'Right, then,' Walsh rapped, twisting the man round to
check the belt tying his wrists before moving to the front,
'I'm taking you in to Limehouse nick.'

'What for!'

'Absolute bodily harm, attempted rape and threatening
to murder—just for starters.'

'I need a bloody doctor!'

'Too bad, *mate*.' He started the car but paused when
Kate touched his arm. 'What's wrong? Don't tell me you're
sorry for the sod.'

'Ha! The more he suffers the better.'

'What, then?'

'It's this thing of being in the public eye. Notoriety. *ITN
Reporter in Rape Ordeal.* All that stuff. And for sure there'll
be implications of irresponsibility—that I somehow
brought the assault on myself.'

Walsh had switched off and was eyeing her. 'OK, girlie,
I can understand all that. But against it, there's the aspect
of public duty—your duty to bring this bastard to justice

—to get him off the streets, even get him some sort of treatment.'

'Jack!' She checked, hands gripped tight to hold back her pent-up distress. 'Sorry. I'm very sorry, but it has to be this way. You're right, of course, but I simply can't go through with it.' Then, topping his further protest: 'Apart from anything else, there's the copycat aspect. How do you expect me to go on the air night after night thinking of all the freaks like him sitting out there with their sick fantasies— thinking maybe they'll—ugh, they'll have a go where he failed! No, Jack, I'm sorry, but that's it.'

The copper grunted in apparent acceptance, started up and drove without further comment to the London Hospital. He parked in the area outside Casualty, then got out and heaved the injured man roughly on to the ground while he unstrapped the belt.

'Just this once, thanks to the lady, you get a breather. But don't you dare get clever and try anything else, 'cos I'll have you sure as day follows night. I've got your prints on that hammer. So just be sure not to get any more stupid than you've been already.' He heaved him up to his feet, glared with contempt into his sullen face a moment, then abruptly kneed him once again in the genitals. As the man doubled forward in renewed agony, he pushed him towards the entrance to Casualty and got back into the car.

'Listen, Jack, about charging the bastard—'

'No.' He gestured her to silence. 'Not another word about it.' He started up and drove out on to the Mile End Road, heading east to get her cleaned up at his home. 'After all, sweetheart, we both know the real reason for your coyness is because you don't want that sentimental, over-protective live-in fiancé of yours finding out.'

Kate groaned, opening the window and leaning out to vomit heartily on to the road.

'You know, Foxy,' she muttered when she'd at last finished heaving, 'for an ex-copper, you can be quite perceptive.'

*

Taff's frown hung around on and off all the way out of London, along the M40 and into his office. He knew of course that it stemmed from the sense of unease born of his anxieties the previous evening. It had been so acute that, even after the phone call from Dell to say guess what, there's a lovely girl here who wants a word, and thence to the girl herself, hugely apologetic for not leaving him a message on the Ansaphone but anyway, knowing she was with Papa Walsh, he really shouldn't have worried—even after that call, he had continued to fret. Kate's tone had been too shrill and artificially bright. And why, since it was a set routine between them, had she failed to leave him that message? Dell's earlier anxiety had spoken loud and clear of the tension she had read in Jack's tone. So just what the hell had happened?

Kate had been by no means herself when she finally got home and, pleading acute migraine, had dosed herself up with Codis and dived for bed. Nor had she been any more forthcoming this morning when he'd hurried back up to the flat to ask about the smashed driver's window in her Polo. Really, as a reporter schooled in deception, she could be a lousy liar. But why? Just what happened to cause her to lie?

'Motorway problems again, sir?'

'No worse than usual.' He avoided eye contact with the sergeant. 'What's new on the Marlbury murder? There should be some prelims from the pathologist by now.'

'Not with their staff shortages.'

'Bloody marvellous, isn't it.' He crossed to leave. 'Phone and tell the IO I'm on the way down there now. We promised the news ghouls a look at the grave.'

In the event, it was late morning before he got back to Kidlington and got the message to contact the ITN news editor.

'Belatedly returning your call, Lawrence.' Taff's casual tone concealed a storm of anxiety. 'What's the problem?'

'Are we free to speak in confidence, old lad?'

'OK this end.' Taff reached to switch on a tape-recorder. 'Why?'

'I feel you deserve a word of explanation about our Kate. Also, to some extent, an apology.'

'I'm listening.'

There was a brief pause, and Taff caught the muted sounds of Cawley lighting up one of his mini cigars. 'I don't need to tell you how obstinate she can be.' Another pause, this time to inhale smoke. 'Take it from me, I've done my level best to get her off this Aristotle Edwards story. I mean, it's patently fraught with risks and hazards. Trouble is, Bella Edwards virtually refuses to trust anyone but Kate. Certainly there's no way she's going to have the same rapport with anyone else on our team. Moreover, as Kate sees it, she's been on board with this one all along.'

Another pause, Taff getting increasingly twitched. 'So?'

'The thing is, any normal person might have been expected to learn a lesson from that ghastly business last night. But wouldn't you know it, with our Kate—well it's just hardened her determination. In fact, I have to say—'

'What—hang on a moment—what ghastly business is this exactly?'

'Ah . . .'

'In detail please, Lawrence.'

There was a theatrical pause before the editor breathed out the expletive. 'Ohhhhh shit. I thought you knew.'

CHAPTER 7

'In detail, Jack, with no edits.' Taff scowled at his onetime governor. Not that the lack of trust detracted from his affection for the man; he had always known him as Foxy, after all, accepting the deviousness as a dimension of the detective whom, in so many ways, he regarded as a substitute father. The emotion was mutual. Nor had Taff's disinterest in Heather Walsh caused any bad feeling between them, Dell having early on set that one to rest.

'Don't they give you blokes any work to do? When I was a DCI there was no way I could have just pushed off and left the desk empty.'

'Except when the pubs were open, eh? Anyway, I have a reliable team in whose hands I'm happy to leave the ship.'

It wasn't necessarily true; the reliability of Sergeant Warboys was an unknown quantity. But needs must. Lawrence Cawley's gaffe had finally forced the issue. The phoney war was over; the pretence of sitting on the fence and browsing through the trial transcript was now finished. To hell with his scruples over the Met, Taff was now committed.

'Kate was lured into a trap on the pretence of meeting up with Mandy Trotter.'

'So whoever set the trap is also probably responsible for Mandy's disappearance.'

Walsh nodded. 'She tried to reach me on the car-phone, meanwhile making her way to the rendezvous.'

'At?'

'St Katherine's Dock area.' He paused, sitting back. 'Look, Taff, why don't we go down the boozer and talk this through, eh?'

'Because there isn't time. Go on.'

'She finally got through to me, but as she rang off some ape smashed her car window and dragged her off down an alley. No, no, relax. You know your Katie. She kept her head, chose the moment and put in the knee, then whacked him silly with his own hammer. But that wasn't the end of it, poor love. When she got back to her car, no keys. Then, while she was looking for them, somebody else in what we think was a Range-Rover, tried to run her down. Luckily, Uncle Jack arrived just in time to see off the second fella.'

'Diawl . . .' Taff was thinking of his girl and the monumental show she'd put on for him the previous evening to try and appear casual—also trying to recall what on earth, in his own anxious state, he had said to her. 'A migraine, Jack, that's what she told me. After an ordeal like that!'

'Kid's got bottle all right.' Then, abruptly: 'Listen, it honestly wasn't her fault. She did all the right things. By the grace of God, she wasn't physically injured. Deeply shocked, of course. But, worse even than that, Taff, she's utterly paranoid about you finding out.'

'Yeah? Really tactful guy, that editor of hers.'

'What I'm saying, lad, she braced herself up like a lion last night to keep it from you. So, OK, just do the big thing, give her a break and pretend you don't know about it.'

'Big thing bollocks, Jack. I'm going after them. End of discussion. I agree, she's suffered more than enough without me giving her a hard time as well. But from now on, I'm on board.'

Arnold Grundi woke with a start to find the woman standing beside his bed. She held a tired bunch of asters clasped in token sympathy before her bosom. She was dressed up like it was disco time, the musky smell of her perfume hitting the hospital ward hard enough to rouse the dead. Not that Arnold found the scent any more attractive than the woman or the flowers. Any other woman, yes, within reason; but not this particular specimen at this moment of extreme vulnerability.

The ward had only four beds in it, one empty, the next containing an elderly man so frail he looked unreal, the other occupied by a drunken vagrant so deeply out he would have slept through the last trumpet. No prospect of any help from either of them.

'How'd you know I was here, Maureen?'

'A certain angry gent with a special interest in the state of your health—he told me, Arnie.' She slapped the flowers sharply across his face as if they were a flagellate's whip. 'He had some very spiteful things to say about you.' Again the flowers whipped across, this time slashing mercilessly across the medical dressings covering his damaged head. 'Also some very cutting things to say about me—for being such a dumb twat as to choose you!'

This time the flowers whacked on to his loins, drawing a gasp of agony in response.

'Lay off, will yer, Maureen. I took a lot of punishment down there.'

'Nothing to what you're going to get if the man catches up with you.' However, she dumped the flowers aside and dragged up a chair so as to sit beside him. 'Our Miss Lewis wallop you one down there? Found your tender spot, did she?'

She slid her hand in under the sheets and, to his horror, started massaging his tackle.

'Stop that, will yer!'

'Why, Arnie? You was never coy before.'

'I've got to lay off it,' he groaned. 'That's what the doc said. Nothing for at least a month.' Then as she persisted, her painted face stretched in a malicious grin: 'Stop it, Maureen! You want to do for me!'

'Yes, you bungling prat, I do!' She hung on as he tried desperately to fend her off. 'Sort you out once and for all!'

'They'll crucify you, Taff old son. The moment they find out you're sniffing around the Edwards case, they'll have your guts for garters. And not just the Met but your Thames Valley masters as well. It doesn't matter how much cause you've got or what evidence you dig up, you're on a dead loser.'

'You think I don't know that, Jack? I've heard it twice already from Hammond and Barker.'

'So leave it to me,' Walsh snapped, tearing the wrapper off a stick of gum. 'Just because I left the force doesn't mean I'm over the bloody hill!'

Taff was on the point of remarking how inept Walsh had been as Kate's minder the previous evening. However, he managed to leave it unsaid, instead pulling out a list of priorities he'd jotted down. 'All right then, so instead of wasting time, try and be of some help. Like, number one, how do I get to see the Edwards case file?'

Walsh groaned and grumbled a bit more before finally

acquiescing. He had known all along there'd be no talking
Taff out of it, moreover that the lad had no alternative but
to go in totally naked. It was no good, for instance, trying
to cover himself by confiding in his immediate guv'nor or
in their chiefie. Whatever their sympathies for Taff and his
latest cause, it would be impossible for either of them to
authorize a covert inquiry outside Thames Valley limits.
They'd have to take it upstairs, ultimately to their Chief
Constable who would in turn be obliged to refer it to the
Metropolitan Chief Commissioner—who could hardly be
expected merely to sit on it.

'There's a sergeant I know fairly well in the Admin Support Unit.' He keyed the file for Yard personnel up on to
the screen. 'Here he is, Harvey Bolt. Works in the ASU's
Central Bureau.'

'Any particular reason why Sergeant Bolt should risk life
and limb by leaking me the hard-copy file? That is, assuming Hammond and Barker haven't already managed to get
the whole lot shredded.'

'Well—' Walsh shrugged, mildly embarrassed at
revealing the extent of his internal Yard network—'for starters, he's done me some hefty indiscretions in the past, so
he can hardly refuse to meet you. The rest's down to you.
Offer him the right deal, he'll oblige.' He reached for the
phone and tapped out the number. 'You'll find him a bit
of a stroppy bastard. Stuck there in ASU, for whatever
reason, and reckons he's been passed by for promotion. Not
much new in that, eh. The Yard's full of them.'

Harvey Bolt had the sturdy, barrel-chested build of a
parade-ground chiefie—hardly the physique suited to key-
board filing or the librarian duties of the ASU. Taff recognized him as he came into the St Anne's Lane pub only
because of the off-duty uniform of a navy-blue anorak over
sports jacket, blue serge trousers and pale-blue shirt. Both
men exchanged weather and traffic chat until they were
settled with pints in the corner.

'Thanks for meeting me.'

'I wouldn't have, sir, if it had been anyone else but Mr Walsh asking.' He took a pull of ale, wiped his moustache, then added: 'You're bad news at the Yard.'

'I'm not into any sort of anti-Met crusade, I assure you. It's purely circumstantial.'

Bolt shrugged dismissively. 'Not for me to pass judgement. You make your own bed.' He gave him a sidelong wink. 'With, if I may say so, a very attractive bedfellow.'

Taff, although he managed to subdue his irritation, resented the assumption of bias on his part when in reality Kate had always been secondary to his Yard troubles—or, damn it, she had until now.

'Mr Walsh said you're interested in the back files on the Aristotle Edwards case.' Then, at Taff's nod: 'What's the problem?'

'You really want to know?'

Bolt eyed him in surprise, wiping each side of his moustache as if to clear away confusion. 'You can hardly expect me to leak you the goods without being satisfied it's right and proper so to do.'

'Fine.' To some extent, Taff felt reassured. Better this, perhaps, than a strictly commercial deal. 'There's strong evidence to suggest a miscarriage of justice.'

'Don't you believe it, guv. The sod's as guilty as hell.'

'If so, why are the two IOs so desperate to prevent the case being reopened?'

Bolt shrugged and took another pull of ale. 'Both of them got promotion out of it. Commander Hammond in particular has a lot to lose.'

'So has my fiancée,' Taff remarked, seeing no alternative but to confide in the man. 'She had a witness who made a statement to the PCA incriminating Superintendent Barker. The witness duly disappeared into thin air. Then last night, Miss Lewis was lured to a phoney rendezvous, grossly assaulted and warned off.'

Bolt's expression was closed and stony. He shook his head, rubbing again at his moustache as Taff continued: 'Granted, there's no direct proof that either officer's behind these events. But they've both tried to pressure me to influence Kate. And it's also hard to see how anyone but them could have known about the advent of this new witness. They're not proven guilty, Sergeant, but in my view there's a sufficiently strong case to warrant further investigations.' Taff nodded. 'By me—with, right now, some help from you.'

Still the man hesitated, obstinacy in every line of his face. No wonder they pass you over for promotion, Taff thought unfairly. 'And the guv'nor,' Bolt remarked, draining his pint and placing it prominently for a refill, 'obviously, he agrees with that evaluation else he wouldn't have contacted me.'

'Like me, Mr Walsh is exceedingly choked about the attack on Kate.'

'Ah yes.' Bolt nodded stolidly. 'Makes a difference, of course, when it gets personal.'

'Not to the extent of clouding my judgement, Sergeant.'

There was a pause, Bolt eyeing his empty pint. Taff took it for a refill. When he came back, the Admin man had produced a large envelope. 'What's the deal if I let you have this?'

Taff hesitated, wondering if he expected money. If not, it would be a huge tactical error to offer it.

'If whatever you give me eventually leads to a collar, you get the credit, OK?'

Bolt snorted in contempt. 'Along with the sack for breaching standing orders. Thanks a bunch.'

'What else had you in mind?'

'There's a lot of fat cats filling those upper-storey offices at the Yard,' he remarked dourly. 'Hammond's typical of them. If you and Mr Walsh can manage to get me transferred to C-Ten, that's a department which could give me a lot of job satisfaction.'

Ah yes, Taff thought, that figures: internal complaints— giving him the chance to take vengeance on all these perceived fat cats. Hardly the most ideal motivation. But right now Taff was in no mood to argue. He wanted that envelope—along with anything else the sergeant could unearth.

'I can't guarantee C-Ten, of course. But you'll have shown the right spirit by cooperating in this one.' He grinned but got no response. Irony was not apparently Bolt's forte. 'What's in there?'

'Since all the original stuff dates from the mid-'eighties, it's been filed on microfiche.' He tapped the envelope. 'That's what I've repro'ed for you in here—mainly witness statements, forensic reports and so on. Likewise various photo exhibits. But there's some other stuff, later presumably, which is stored on disc. If you tell me what you want, I'll search through and bring you a print-out of whatever. How about the trial? The entire transcript's on microfiche as well, but . . .'

'I've already got it. In fact, there was one thing came out of the transcript which you might be able to help with. There's a reference during Barker's cross-examination where he was asked about the identity of his principal informant. Naturally, he pleaded privilege. However, it was agreed he should show the judge documented evidence about the informant.'

The sergeant frowned, shaking his head. 'There's only one informant in this lot and he's some geezer called Alfie Small who grassed Edwards up on remand.'

'No, not Small. No one else?'

'Not in with this lot.'

'Damn.' Taff thought a moment, then pointed. 'Even so, you might be able to find out the name from the informants' fund.'

'You're kidding.'

'The chances are he was paid. Info on a murder has got to be worth a fair whack. In which case, his name'll be there in the fund file. Probably around the end of August 1985 when the body was found and the investigation got under way.'

Bolt was deeply twitched, shaking his head, fussing his moustache. 'It's outside the bureau.'

'But inside ASU—I think.'

The sergeant gave a reluctant nod. 'Even so, people are likely to wonder.'

Taff gave him a cheerful wink. 'Think of C-Ten—that should help you come up with something.' He stood up and took the envelope. 'I'm heading for the Yard, but we'd best walk there by different routes.'

'The Yard, sir?'

Taff laughed at his open concern. 'I may be unpopular with the Met; that doesn't mean I'm *persona non grata*. The fact is, there's an inspector I know moderately well in C-Ten. I'll go and chat him up about you.'

'But surely . . .'

'I won't mention your name at this stage, don't worry— only when we hit lucky. My main object is to be *seen* around the place—best of all, whispering to one of the C-Ten spooks. With any luck, that should start a few rumours and put the wind up Messrs Barker and Hammond.'

'Katie darling, come and sit down.' The editor went way over the top by fetching her a chair to sit beside him at the big oval news desk.

'I may be bruised, Lawrence, I'm not crippled.'

'You're as mad as Kate Adie. You should be on a week's sick leave.' Then, more solicitously: 'Seriously, love, how are you?'

Kate lowered herself gingerly on to the chair and grinned at him, undeceived. 'Since by far the worst of my bruises is the one on my knee, just imagine what state Rent-a-Rape's in this morning.'

'Speaking as a red-blooded male, I'd rather not.'

You mean, speaking as a cold-blooded poof, Kate thought; but then, even gays have goolies. She waited while he lit up one of his little cheroots, wondering just what game he was playing with all the sociability and charm.

'Seriously, Katie, there's a strong chance of delayed shock or whatever. Why don't you at least take a couple of days' break—call it convalescent leave, eh.'

'No chance.' In fact, nothing could have held more appeal for her than a good rest. She felt absolutely lousy: bruised, grazed, hungover and shaky; everything about her screamed out for rest and comfort. 'If I take a sudden break, Taff's going to want to know why. The effort I went to last night to act normal and hide it from him, there's no way I'm going to risk taking time off.'

'Katie, listen . . .'

'No, he'd got absolutely spare if he found out—could even go walkabout, knowing Taff. He's hyper-sensitive about my taking any risks—' She checked, noting the editor's expression, pointing at him in rising horror. 'Lawrence, I don't believe it . . .'

'Look, how was I to know you hadn't told him?'

'Basic, that's how!' She was on her feet now, glaring down at him in rage and betrayal, all too familiar with his perfidy. 'You devious, cunning sod! Just determined to trick him in, weren't you! Bastard!'

'Katie darling, on my life—'

'*Liar!!*'

CHAPTER 8

Taff frowned in uncertainty. He was sure Mandy Trotter's flat was on the ground floor five along from the end, but now, trying to get in by the back way, he found it locked. He checked the doors on either side just in case, then went round and clambered up on the railing to peer in through the front ground-floor window. Between the looped net curtains he was able to make out the massed ranks of cuddlies, at least confirming he'd got the right flat. So someone had locked the door and, from what he could see through the front window, had also turned out the lights and cleared away the bits of broken china pig from the floor.

It was while Taff was straining to see in that he realized an elderly lady was eyeing him from next door. He hopped

off the railing and went along to talk, glad that he'd
replaced his uniform tunic with a tweed jacket.

'Hello, we spoke a couple of evenings ago—about Miss
Trotter.'

The woman frowned. 'Really?'

'Well, in fact, you spoke to the young lady I was with.'

'Ah yes, the TV person.' She smiled in recollection. 'The
black girl hasn't been back. Or at least, not so far as I am
aware.'

'Someone has.' Taff nodded towards the window. 'It's
been tidied up in there and the backdoor locked. The land-
lord, perhaps.'

'Ah, out of the question. Idle sloth.' She frowned. 'Maybe
it was her—maybe she just popped back to, er, collect a
Teddy or two. She does live a rather, let's say, irregular
life.'

'Doing what, do you know?'

'Well . . .' the woman eyed him askance—'obviously,
you'll be with the television people as well. In fact, come
to think of it, you do look rather like that Ian McShane.
No? Well, in any event, one has to be circumspect. Let's
say she's in hostessing.'

'Why not?' Taff gave her an Ian McShane wink. 'After
all, one man's hostess is another man's, er . . .'

'Plaything?'

'Spot on.' He scribbled her his home and work numbers.
'If you see her on anyone else in the place, I'd be grateful
if you'd let me know.' Then, thinking better of it, he altered
the work number to ITN's and told her to contact Kate.
Best to be discreet. It was one thing to try and put the wind
up Barker and Hammond by openly chatting up C-Ten
officers at the Yard, but actively pursuing unauthorized
investigations in Met-land was something else.

But *diawl*, he thought as he headed back to his car, there's
no denying the thrill: start to get stuck into an investigation
again, get your teeth back into some good solid detection
work, and you realize how bloodless PR is by comparison.
For all the legwork and false starts and tedium, there's

nothing to beat it. Once a detective, always a detective, and to hell with retraining as a fat-cat lawyer!

The offices of Randi Dubois were a lot less upmarket than his flamboyant style had led Kate to expect. Basically, they amounted to a converted shop off the Brixton Road, its partitions DIY, its fittings MFI, its décor naff. Only the secretary was impressive—as a possible Miss West Indies if not as a shorthand-typist.

'Someone's in there with him, miss. Care to wait?'

'He was expecting me. Kate Lewis of ITN.'

'I'll check, OK.'

She did so on the intercom and immediately the partition door flew open.

'Come on in here, Katie baby.' Randi beckoned her in as if to a party. 'Someone here I figure maybe you met before.'

She might, of course, have guessed who it was. None the less it knocked her sideways to see his grin across the room.

'Hi, Kate. How you feeling?'

'Taff . . .' She shook her head, a rush of guilt and embarrassment competing with a rising sense of resentment. 'That bastard of an editor!'

'Forget it, OK.'

'You realize he leaked it—about the assault—you realize he leaked it to you deliberately.'

'It figures.'

'Hey, kids,' Randi cut in, 'what's all the rap?'

'It's personal,' Kate told him, still unable to raise a smile. 'The point is, Chief Inspector Roberts shouldn't be here.'

'The man told me he's part of the team,' the lawyer protested. 'And believe me, the way things are moving right now, we sure need a cop on board.'

'OK, so we'll discuss this later,' Taff remarked firmly before resuming to the lawyer. 'Tell Kate about the latest from the Yard.'

'In fact,' Randi corrected, 'the word came from the Complaints Authority about the response they've been getting from the yard. Would you believe, up until yesterday, the signals said we were definitely going to get some action.'

'Oh?'

'The DPP had instructed the Met to reopen the investigation prior to a possible retrial.' Randi grimaced, shaking his head in irony. 'But by one of those strange little coincidences, no sooner had Miss Mandy Trotter disappeared than the Yard came back to the PCA wanting a further statement from her.'

'Bastards!'

'Damn sure, that's how it looks, yeah. Mega bastards.' He grimaced again. 'So what's new, huh? This is a crappy game we're in and up against some very slippery people.' The lawyer checked, swinging to Taff. 'No offence to the Thames Valley force, Chief. They're angels by comparison with certain elements in the Met.'

Taff shrugged. Whereas he fully agreed, he was damned if he'd ever say so to Dubois.

'So anyway,' Randi resumed, 'I now have the PCA asking me to produce our witness, and I'm having to tell them so sorry, but Ms Trotter's suddenly vanished. The Authority's attitude is, well, too bad, fella, if you can't produce her or else demonstrate foul play over her disappearance, then there's no valid new evidence and no grounds for any damn thing whatsoever. Tough on you and goodbye.'

He grimaced again, then turned to gesture towards the coffee flask in the corner; but Kate shook her head, grim and dispirited.

'I have to tell you,' the lawyer added, 'I got strong indications from the PCA that unless we can actually walk Mandy in there, they do *not* want to know. So far as they're concerned, you and ITN took them for a ride—'

'Terrific!'

'They reckon you were in conspiracy with Bella Edwards to pull yet another stunt in her FAME campaign.' Then, waving down Kate's angry protest, he added: 'OK, it's too bad, but you can't blame them for reading it that way.'

It was as she and Taff were leaving that Randi mentioned

another irony. 'The Legal Aid Board finally agreed to pay
my fees. Up till now, they've been dragging their feet in the
way they always do over applications. Of course it has to
be just another of those strange little coincidences, but the
same day we lose our witness along with our whole darned
case, up they pop with the approval.'

The little coincidences continued. Over all the years Jack
Walsh had been building up his security network at Klein
Holdings, he had only once before had any hassle from the
Yard. By no element of chance, that raid had coincided
with his giving Taff some help at prying into various City
firms—in the process unwittingly trespassing on the toes of
the Serious Fraud Squad.

On this occasion, Jack Walsh was just phoning round his
East End contacts in quest of a certain lower-league villain
and grass called Alfie Small when the door of his office was
opened by a very flustered secretary. She was barely one
step ahead of a sergeant and a PC from Records clutching
a search-and-seize warrant.

'Jack Ian Walsh, we have reason to believe you have
been accessing into the police computer network for the
purpose of illegally extracting information from, among
other sources, CRO and the DVLC.'

Since this was substantively true, Walsh jumped up with
a show of outrage, told the secretary she could leave and
then reminded the sergeant of the extreme technical chal-
lenges involved in trying to prove computer fraud and network prying of this ilk.

'Having said which, lads, and having satisfied myself
re the authenticity of this warrant, I shall endeavour to
cooperate as best I can with your inquiries.'

'Don't take the piss, chief. We don't like having to close
you down, but that's the score. All your discs and the bulk
of this hardware, OK?'

'Just tell me one thing: who's behind it? Who's putting
in the boot this time?'

'You know they wouldn't tell us that.' The sergeant

seemed genuinely sorry about it. 'You can try asking our
guv'nor by all means. You might get lucky.'

'But right now, you two are here to put up the shutters.'

'That's the size of it, yes.'

With which they started systematically itemizing and
then stripping the place, for all the world as if it was a
warehouse full of hard-porn videos.

Kate held back until Taff had parked outside the FAME
community centre, then she touched his arm. 'Let's just get
us sorted first. You and me.'

He paused with a show of reluctance, the door part open
and one foot out, but none the less aware they had to talk
it through. 'The decision's made, love.'

'Like hell it is, *love*, because this could well cost you your
job. There's no chance your Thames Valley bosses'll wear
it. So it's got to be career suicide. Damn sure I'd rather
pack in the whole stupid story than see you jeopardize the
last fifteen years of your life just because of this Edwards
nonsense.'

He went to respond, but she persisted: 'No, listen to
me, it's not only your career, it's *us* as well. That was the
agreement, remember? To keep our two jobs totally separate. So it's no good saying that because I got lured into a
bit of bother with a mugger, you've got to come charging
in like the US Cavalry. That's no reason, Taff. Our life
together is more important than that.'

Again she cut off his response, this time gripping his hand
in hers. 'Us, us, us! You and me and everything we mean
to each other. Damn Lawrence Cawley and his blessed
story! To hell with crucifying Barker and Hammond! To
hell with winning justice for Aristotle Edwards, if that's
really what it's about!' She pressed his hand to her cheek.
'Taff, I love you and I want us to be as we are—as we were
until last night—or until my beloved editor put his damned
oar in this morning!'

Suddenly she was shaking and, to her chagrin, felt her
eyes welling with tears. Delayed shock, no doubt, her head

still heavy and woollen, but it still wasn't her style. He went
to kiss her, but she pushed him away, snuffling into a hanky
and muttering to leave her alone.

Taff sighed, thinking how much easier it would have been
had she come blazing in at him as usual. By coming on all
earnest and weepy like this she made him feel she really
could pack it all in if he got obstinate.

In the event, his dilemma was cut short by a call on his
car-phone: Jack Walsh duly telling him of the raid by the
two spooks from the Yard and warning him to be sure and
watch his back.

'Man, I'm sorry! The rotten buggers. Who was it actually
applied for the warrant?'

'Some CI in Records called Smythe. No doubt one of
Barker's toadies.'

'Right. So what now, Jack? Are you OK to keep after
Alfie Small for us?'

'Why not? They cut off my electronics, not my head.'

Taff grunted as he rang off, then turned decisively to his
girl. 'The last straw, love. They bloody threaten me, they
get vicious with you, and now they've cracked down on
Jacko.' He moved to get out of the car. 'As you said, damn
your editor and to hell with winning justice for Edwards.
No, it's those two Met bastards I'm after.'

It took Bella no time at all to generate a massive head of
stream over their rebuff from the Police Complaints Authority. She must, Kate thought, have been drinking or else
was high on some other form of stimulant. Surely she
couldn't get quite so fired up by what was merely the latest
in a string of Whitey Establishment evasions. But fired up
she was: spluttering and inarticulate, raging around the
office, all but beating her ample breast.

Worse, noticing that Taff was in uniform beneath the
tweed jacket, her frustration focused on him.

'You never told me! Hiding a thing like that!'

'Hiding nothing, Bella. He just happens to be my boyfriend?'

'But the Law, for God's sake . . .'

'So? If he'd been an accountant or a dentist or whatever, you couldn't have expected me to say it when I introduced him, so why should a policeman be any different?'

Kate well knew it was a futile comparison. To the likes of Bella, there was a world of difference—a world born of prejudice, the suss laws, victimization and a whole culture of oppression. People in her world did not join the police or respect them or trust them. There existed an unbridge-able them-and-us gulf dividing them.

Besides, no matter how vigorous the Met's community-liaison efforts, it was more profitable to Bella, both in terms of FAME donations and electoral votes, to emphasize that gulf. If ever the *Filth* became the *Clean*, Bella would risk losing a great deal of her popular support. Like so many others who won power and prestige from the race-ralations industry, she depended on society's remaining divided. And what better rallying point for that division than the police reputation for racial prejudice?

Taff made no attempt to intervene. He knew from first-hand experience what was involved: the legacy of hatred no less than the vested interest in sustaining it. If Katie could patch up some sort of alliance, then, fair enough, he'd go along with it. But it was down to her, not him.

Kate did her best. She pointed out that they didn't *know* Mandy's actual fate—that the girl could indeed have bottled out of her own accord and sought refuge with her Gulf daddy—so it was no good Bella's demanding air time or mounting hysterical anti-pig demonstrations until they could be sure. But the black woman remained implacable. She had glimpsed an end to the tunnel—smelt the prospect of a retrial and the release of her poor wronged husband—and was beyond logic.

'To hell with all your fine reasons, Miss Lewis: you do seven years without your man and see how reasonable you feel!'

One of the more suspect prosecution witnesses singled out

by Taff from the trial transcript was a prostitute called
Doris Haig. To their relief, they found she was still living
at the address recorded on her statement in the case file. It
was a council flat in Camberwell, its front door in dire need
of paint, as was the face of the woman who opened up to
their knock. She wore only a Chinese-silk drape, apparently
having come straight from her bed.

'Ms Haig?'

'Who's asking?' But then, recognizing Kate, her attitude
promptly transformed, ushering them inside to her luxuri-
ously furnished living-room. Now in her late thirties, Doris
Haig may well have been clinging on to a younger woman's
profession, but she was as yet a long way from having to
curtail her lifestyle. Nothing but the best in rugs, décor and
china; all the latest in hi-fi; quality brandy and liqueurs in
the cabinet; real carnations and lilies in the cut-crystal
vases. Who needs paint on the front door, Kate thought, if
it opens on to such glittering riches.

'Word got around you was doing a show on the trade,'
Doris remarked, settling them into her Harrods best.

'Really?'

'Been sussing it out with Angel Mendoza, so we heard.'

'You're not one of his girls, are you?'

''Course not. Gross pig.' Then, less tartly as she lit up a
Turkish cigarette: 'It's a tight little world, you know, Miss
Lewis. We all try to keep up with what's going on. The
gossip vine, savvy? There'd be a lot of interest in a show
like that.'

Kate blinked, wondering just what sort of a show the
trade had cultivated on the vine. Compared with most pro-
fessions, it did seem to have a rather limited scope for
variety, albeit of compelling interest to the young and with
possibilities for the Olympics.

'Sorry to disappoint you, but we're here about the evidence you gave at the Ari Edwards's trial.'

Doris blinked and exhaled smoke like a plump blonde
dragon, her dishevelled charm promptly hardening to ice.
'What the hell . . . ?'

'You know ITN: the slot for justice and the underdog.'

'Bollocks.' She shook her head, plomping down into a chair, the drape clasped tightly around her. Clearly her charms, such as remained of them, were reserved for cash-only transactions. 'If you're after justice, that's exactly what that brutal swine got. A life-sentence was too kind for him! They should of topped the sod for what he done to poor little Arlene. Bloody torturer, that's what!'

'Was that why you perjured yourself at the trial?' Taff asked quietly.

'Perjured my arse, Sunny Jim!' She gestured in contempt at him. 'Here, who is this burk? Some sort of clever sod, is he? Well, I tell you this, mate, you can just perjure off, asking questions like that. What I told the jury at that trial was *true* and no mistake. I saw the black ape humping her out the door and across to his car. Had her over his shoulder, he did, and all tied up in them black plastic bin liners. At the time, I thought it was a carpet or a rug or something. But there was no doubt in my mind whatsoever later on. The moment I heard they'd pulled that poor kid's corpse out from them foundations down Newington way, I *knew* it for bleeding certain. That was *her* he was lugging out the place that night, I said to meself. No sodding rug in them bags: that was poor little Arlene Milton over his shoulder or I'm a Dutch uncle.'

She certainly didn't look in the least avuncular, Kate thought, her coarsened features and lank over-dyed hair lending her more the look of a French aunt.

'What were you doing so far from your normal beat?'

Doris scowled and offered Taff some crisp advice, but he persisted. 'You said in court that you were working Dove Street, but that was a couple of miles from your normal beat in Shepherd Market. How come?'

'Don't know much about the game, do you, Sunny. The fact of it is, I was working the taxis. Just chance I was dropped off down there.'

'Why didn't the driver take you back to your normal pitch? That's the routine.'

'Because I got out with the punter, that's why. I felt like a change, OK.'

'Dead risky, trespassing like that, Doris. You could have got your face laid open for that.'

'Here, Miss Lewis, what's your toy-boy think he's up to, eh? I'm not taking this shit from him.'

'On the contrary,' Taff persisted, 'you're the one talking shit. You're lying now and you lied when you told the court you'd seen Ari Edwards that night!'

'No! Why? Why should I lie? Wasn't nothing in it for me to tell lies!'

'On the contrary, you had a great deal at stake. Quite apart from the vengeance aspect, you'd been put under a lot of pressure by the Filth in the person of your friend Mr Barker.'

'Barker's no friend of mine, mate! That big, over-blown turd's not worth a used Johnnie!' Then, in renewed retaliation: 'Anyway, what's that you was saying about vengeance?'

'Every tom on the streets wanted vengeance,' Taff rapped out. 'The moment word got around how savagely she'd been murdered, Ari's stock hit the pit. Bloody hell, even if it wasn't him but a mad client who'd killed her, Arlene was still one of his girls. He should have protected her. What else is a pimp for, if not that! As far as you were concerned, the big bastard had it coming to him. So when Barker came and pressured you to help stitch him, you were quick to go along with it.'

The woman had stubbed out her fag and jumped up in angry rejection. 'Why don't you do us both a favour, Miss Lewis, and get him out of here!'

'Do you deny what he's been saying, Doris?'

'Deny . . . 'course I deny it! Never heard such cods.'

'Strange. You see, we heard it differently from one of Arlene's mates. You'll remember Mandy Trotter. Mandy's in no doubt at all you were lying about seeing Ari. And she has some revealing suggestions about Barker's hold over you.'

*

In the normal course of events, thanks to his network of underworld contacts and the ample funds allowed him by Klein Holdings, Jack Walsh would have expected no problem tracking down the likes of Alfie Small. He already knew the official police side of the man. The pattern of minor burglaries, nearly always of the walk-in type while fronting as a house-decorator, the drift into fencing and then, later on, into informing on the crooks with whom he was in contact—this pattern strongly suggested the opportunist Jack-the-lad type rather than anything heavy like blagging or the gangland scene. Small had no record of violence but had been through the full tariff of court sentences up to a two-year stretch. Predictably enough, the frequency of his convictions had tailed right off since turning grass in the early 1980s. In fact he had avoided the nick altogether since 1985 when, on remand in Brixton Prison, he had met Aristotle Edwards and, so it seemed, wheedled a full confession out of the man. Intriguingly enough, the Crown had seen fit to withdraw the dual charges of burglary and handling when Small appeared in court less than a month after giving evidence of the alleged admission at Ari's Old Bailey trial.

So much for what was known by the police—fortunately established by Walsh in advance of the clamp-down on his operations. As for what was known of the man by the underworld, here again it was a predictable pattern. Born and brought up in Stepney, he was tolerated by the East End villains who regarded him as a relatively harmless operator who played by the rules, doubtless paying his dues and informing the underworld bosses even more diligently than he grassed to the Old Bill.

Walsh had no problem finding out Alfie's favoured haunts, his usual landlady, his local pubs and clubs, even the fence he most often worked with. Everyone who was anyone in the crime business around the Stepney docklands seemed to know Alfie Small. But the one thing no one seemed to know was his present whereabouts. By yet another of those mysterious coincidences, at much the same time that the Mandy Trotter statement hit the Yard, Alfie had gone walkabout.

They met in the Bag o' Nails for a case airing—the ageing general and his erstwhile aide—their mood sombre and bitter.

'Barker and Hammond are playing dirty, guv'nor. They're way out of order.'

'It certainly looks like they're running scared—like they've got more to lose than just a bit of career status. How's our Katie feeling today?'

'It eventually caught up with her—so much so she finally let me take her home and tuck her up in bed.' He eyed the chief askance. 'It strikes me it was a lot worse than she's letting on.' Then, getting no more than a shrug, he added: 'Listen, about your office—I'm really sorry.'

'Forget it.'

'The thing is, I wanted Barker to know that I'm sniffing around the Yard so I put on a little pantomime with a mate of mine from C-Ten.'

'Reckoning to panic the bastard into some action, hm?'

Taff grunted in bitter acknowledgement. 'If only I'd thought about it, I'd have realized he was likely to hit you.' He paused to drink spritzer, then shook his head in resolve. 'I can't promise it'll be quick, but I'll bloody well get things back to normal for you eventually.'

Walsh chuckled, poking at him in mock rebuke. 'It's cheap at the price, son. Much more of my boring routine at Klein's, I'd have been brain-dead. Talking of which, although Alfred John Small appears to have gone to ground, I've put out the equivalent of a contract on him. The second he comes up for air, he'll get an offer he can't refuse and come running.'

'Yeah? Still the man of influence, then.'

'Too right.' He raised his glass in a wry toast. 'Seems I can do everything except make you laugh.'

Taff snorted in irony. 'The fact is, I've taken the pledge:

no more hilarity until I've nailed those two bastards to the wall.' He returned the toast, however, allowing a dour grin. 'What we need here for our system of appeals is the French method of an examining magistrate to review new evidence.'

'Tell that to the Runciman Commission.'

'Sure—' Taff pulled a face—'and end my career in the process. But look how much more sensible it would have been for Kate just to wheel Mandy Trotter in front of an examiner instead of having to go down the PCA route.'

Walsh grunted, nibbling some peanuts before remarking: 'I thought I'd run a check on Lystons, the big hotel and property chain who own Blandells Casino.'

Taff nodded approval. 'Referred to in the trial transcript as supplying the bulk of Arlene's clients.'

Walsh grinned, one foxy eyebrow raised in irony. 'The word is, some of those clients were very highly placed, politicians among them, and as such, they're determined to prevent a retrial.'

'Ah. The *Eye*'s Cabinet Bimbo brigade whom Edwards's defence counsel tried so hard to get into the witness-box.'

'The same, no doubt. The high and the mighty whose esteemed names and reputations Judge Willis protected on the grounds of privilege. You want a bet, my son, I'll offer you ten to one that, no matter how much pressure we're able to put on Barker and Hammond, there's no way the legal Establishment is ever going to allow a retrial.'

CHAPTER 9

The senior officer on gate duty kept the formalities to a minimum. Maybe he was impressed by Taff's warrant card or else knew Randi's reputation for complaining. Whichever, he personally escorted them across to the prison hospital, then instructed the nursing officer on Ari Edwards's landing to leave them with him for as long as they required.

For a while, until satisfied the officer was no longer within earshot, the heavily bandaged prisoner remained motionless, seeming barely conscious. But then his good eye blinked wide and his good hand reached out to slap Randi's palm as he eased around in the bed to take a closer look at his companion. Abruptly, as he clocked the uniform beneath the tweed jacket, he groaned and relapsed into semi-coma.

'Relax, Ari man, he's OK.' Then, at a further groan, the lawyer added: 'Listen, this is one cop you can trust.'

'Horse shit . . .'

'Don't say that, OK! If you want out, this here's one man could start opening some doors.' He went on to outline Taff's background, then told him of the attack on Kate which had plunged him into action. 'So don't worry, he ain't no crusading do-gooder like me. He's here for strictly personal reasons to do with his lady.'

'In fact,' Taff cut in bluntly, 'I don't give a tinker's damn whether you're innocent or not. I'm just after the two bastards who put you away.'

The reassurance promptly restored Ari to full consciousness, albeit more in belligerence than benevolence.

'Well, that sure as hell figures. That's a cop for you.' He grunted, shaking his head. 'But that don't mean I trust you.'

The lawyer went to protest but Taff waved him aside. 'That goes for both of us, Edwards. I've reviewed the bulk of the evidence, also the transcript of your trial, and so far I've seen nothing to make me think there's been a miscarriage of justice.'

There was a pause, the two men eyeing each other while Randi fidgeted. Finally it was the prisoner who conceded the grunt and the grin. 'Fact of it is, Mr Pig, you and me share the same motive here. You on account of what they done to your TV lady, me 'cos of what they done to my Mandy.' He managed a curt, chesty laugh. 'Makes us a couple of twats, don't it. Two romantic gits.' He turned to hold out a mug for Randi to pour him water from a flask beside the bed, then gestured in concession. 'OK, let's go.'

'Only if you're going to give me the truth. Otherwise we're wasting time.'

'Man, there's no shortage of that in this place. Time, not truth, huh.' Then, more seriously: 'OK, OK, whenever possible, you get the truth. But first—' he pointed cryptically towards the doorway, waiting while Taff shadowed across to confirm there were no prying ears, then he nodded for him to go ahead.

'Suppose we start with these two alleged confessions— the one you signed in the police station and the one you blabbed to Alfie Small in Brixton Prison: how much truth in those?'

'*None.*'

'You sure it wasn't partly true, but the lawyer warned you to make a blanket denial?'

Ari was shaking his head, the visible part of his face sullen with denial. 'They stitched me, Mr Pig, and that's a fact. Stitched me from the start. The very moment they picked me up they was saying the words, telling me what I supposed to have done, telling me they *knew* it was this way and that way 'cos that's how their snout had told them!'

'There was a snout referred to during the trial. They kept him anonymous, but his name was revealed to the judge. You any idea who he was?'

Ari shook his head, pounding his good hand on the bed in agitation. 'You think I haven't asked myself that every day for the last six years?'

Taff gave it a pause for the man to calm down, then switched tack. 'What about what *Private Eye* labelled the Cabinet Bimbo factor? Just how relevant was all that? If the judge had allowed you to name the more élite of Arlene's customers and even call some of them as witnesses, just how much would that have helped your case?'

There was a pause, the black prisoner scowling and fretting against the impulse to lie. 'None,' he grunted at last. 'The opposite, I guess.'

'A bluff, huh,' Randi exclaimed, his fists raised in delight at the way the defence had manipulated the deception. 'A total smokescreen for the jury, huh. Make them think you're a black Robin Hood unable to present your full defence because the whitey judge is blocking your key witnesses. Oh, man, that's cool. That I really dig.'

'Cool like hell,' Ari grumbled. 'It didn't win us the case.'

'No,' Taff agreed. 'And right now it could be killing your chances of getting the case reviewed. Scandal is something no one in high places ever wants. Not the politicians, not the royals—or the bishops or the company chairmen or the chief constables. No matter how safe and above reproach they are themselves, they still have a knee-jerk urge to avoid it. Scandal is the junk food of the popular press. So those at the top repress it at all costs because next time around they could be the target.'

'Listen to him,' Ari chuckled, waving a teasing finger. 'Listen to Mr Preacher!'

'Not preaching, it's a fact of public life.' Taff paused to wave two fingers back at the prisoner in the bed. 'Besides, that key photo the Crown produced at the trial—the one showing Arlene and Janine planting their camera—that suggests *somebody* was photographing the customers *in flagrante* with a view to blackmail. Right?'

'Not me!' The prisoner gestured, shaking his head. 'I had no notion of any damned camera. Believe me, there's no way I'd ever pull a stunt like that. No way!'

'So how come it was there? You provided the girl and the place, so how come—'

'Lystons,' he cut in. 'They provided the customers, mostly from that Blandells Casino of theirs. It had to be them planted the damned thing!'

'And then supplied the Crown with that crucial photograph of Arlene and Janine?'

'Right!'

'But *why*? That photo was vital as confirmation of your alleged motive. Why should Lystons want to frame you?'

The prisoner shrugged, avoiding Taff's gaze. 'They had

to feed someone to the wolves. Who better than a disposable black pimp like old Ari?'

'Lystons?' the lawyer interrupted in surprise. 'You mean *the* Lystons? Hotels and all the rest? One of the UK's biggest companies?'

'Hotels, travel agents, TV company,' Taff listed for him, 'but foremost their gambling empire: betting-shops and casinos.' He turned back to Ari. 'And you made Arlene available to the Blandells customers?'

'Right.'

'Did you tell anyone this before? The police? Your lawyer?'

'I'm not a complete dick-head.' Ari groaned, closing his eyes at the enormity of it. 'You know the outfit Lystons are fronting for? People like that don't piss about. Man, if I'd named Lystons in the witness-box, I'd have been singing my own requiem!'

Taff exchanged a glance with the startled lawyer. Evidently this was way outside Randi's usual league. Nor was it exactly Taff's normal diet, come to that. Organized crime —the Mob, the Triads, *et al.*—these were the province of the Serious Crime Squad at the very least.

'You've named Lystons now. Not in court, I agree, but even so, they're going to put two and two together when I start nosing around.'

But the black prisoner was already shaking his head in dismissal. 'Now it's different. Before all this, I was scared for my life. But not any more. Not now. All I want now is *out*. Just any way you can fix it. Out!'

It was getting on for an hour before they left the prison hospital. By then Ari Edwards was drained of energy, his words slurring, the defiant gleam fading, the fist no longer clenched.

And, to his surprise as he and the lawyer followed their escort back through the evening gloom towards the main gate, Taff found himself half inclined to believe the big pimp—to believe in his innocence of murder, if not much else. There was little rationale to the belief. It was born of those two treacherous parents intuitive impulse and gut feeling; the sort of bastard emotion all shrewd coppers seek to avoid, if only because of its frailty in court.

Yet this time it persisted, taking defiant root in face of all Taff's caution. It mattered, of course. It helped Taff no end because otherwise he ran the risk of hounding a couple of senior coppers who, reacting to the law's heavy presumption of innocence, had taken steps to redress the balance of their case against a guilty man. Reprehensible, no doubt, but something Taff himself had not been above with the evil child molester Leonard Snow. However, if the man was in fact innocent . . .

As they completed the brief check-out formalities, the gate officer jerked a dour thumb towards the exit door. 'Some of your tribe holding an *n'daba* outside, Mr Dubois. Been there since soon after you arrived.'

The tribe, invisible behind the dazzle of TV camera lamps, greeted the two men with the jazzed-up strains of an old battle hymn. Randi's response was more that of a politician than a lawyer, promptly grabbing one of Taff's hands and raising it with his own in a gesture of victory as he joined in with the rousing refrain.

'Chief Inspector Roberts, how's Ari Edwards? Is he badly injured?'

The questions were coming from a TV news reporter, microphone held forward. Beside him, Taff glimpsed the glistening black face of Bella as she pushed forward to grab his other arm.

'Hey, Chief, you reckon you'll be able to help my Ari?'

I'll help you to an early grave, Taff thought, trying to free one or other of his arms so as to evade the intrusive eye of the cameras.

'We had a long and fruitful interview,' Randi babbled at the mike, still hanging firmly on to Taff's arm. 'I guess the Chief Inspector and I would both agree that, in six years of wrongful imprisonment, Ari Edwards was never more hopeful of release than now. Right, Chief?'

Taff had at last pulled free from Bella and, using his free hand to disengage the lawyer's grip, muttered the stock *No Comment* into the out-thrust microphone and ducked sideways out of the pool of light.

Even then it wasn't finished. The FAME team mobbed around him in pretend adulation, trying to hoist him shoulder high for a triumphal march back into the lights which were already swinging after him like remorseless eyes.

In the end Taff had to resort to some determined, below-the-belt tactics in order to disable his admirers sufficiently to break free and make it beyond the traffic barrier, duly racing to the road where he'd parked his car.

Damn them! Damn their inane go-go souls! Setting him up as the victim of a cheap publicity stunt. Anything—any bloody thing at all—to further their damned cause. Well, this time they'd stuck themselves with their own bloody spears because, after this, there was no chance of his getting anywhere near the case! At the very least now, he'd have his chief constable to answer to: *Still off fishing in forbidden waters, Roberts? Still chasing the Met and the limelight?* There was no doubt at all that, by mobilizing the FAME troops for this absurd publicity stunt, Bella had slammed the door both on Taff and on her husband's prospects of freedom. Which, given what a shrewd tactician she was, meant it was almost certainly a deliberate move on her part: she wanted to sabotage Taff's efforts because, secretly, she didn't want her blooming husband out of prison!

'Sorry to leave you to hold the fort all yesterday, Tony. How was it? Many problems?'

Sergeant Warboys gave a wry grin and shook his head. 'Nothing until this morning, as it happens, sir.' He handed over a pile of files on top of which was an internal memo written out in the sergeant's neat hand. *08.43: Chief Supt Marsh requests your presence re BBC-TV exposure last night.*

'Ah . . .'

'The Chief actually looked in here about ten minutes after that, sir. My impression was one of some urgency.'

'Ah . . . Did you by any chance see this TV exposure?'

'As it happens, yes.' He cleared is throat, only half concealing a grin. 'Mrs Warboys and I rather got the impression you'd been set up. My wife remarked that you looked like a gamekeeper turned poacher.'

Taff grunted, shuffling through the pile of files. 'What else?'

'That copy you wanted of the forensic report on the Marlbury murder—lurid colour pics and all.'

'Good.' Taff found the pictures, eyed them briefly, then managed a grin himself as he reached for the phone and tried to dial Kate. Because she had been heavily asleep when he got home the previous evening, he'd waited until this morning to tell her of the FAME demo outside the Scrubs. Then, before dashing off to work, he'd told her to watch the tape he'd recorded later on of the BBC News. Now, to his frustration, he was unable to raise her either at home or at the office or on her car-phone.

In fact, Kate was in the FAME office locked into an eye-balling contest with Bella Edwards.

'Don't lie to me, OK! You're a fraud!'

'Katie, I don't read you here. What you saying?' Bella was dancing around the office, her hands flapping like vestigial wings. 'This ain't the lovely person no more.'

'Too right! This is the betrayed person. You betrayed my boyfriend, you betrayed me!'

'Never, baby!' She attempted to embrace her but Kate fended her off and dodged hurriedly back.

'Don't give me all this Katie baby carnival! When you set up that FAME demo outside the prison last night, you knew exactly what you were doing . . .'

'Celebrating!'

'Bullshit! You betrayed me by getting the Beeb along there! You sabotaged Chief Inspector Roberts's attempts to help the FAME cause—not to mention his career prospects! And in the process you destroyed your husband's chances of freedom!'

'Mad! You gone MAD!' Her yell of fury far exceeded her outburst on finding Taff was a copper. Wailing in fury, she stamped around the room, her head plunging from side to side, her arms flailing the air in frenzied abandon.

Kate watched her in contempt for a while, then moved to leave. Sure enough, before she could reach the door, Bella lunged to grab her, pulling her close. 'See here, why don't you accuse me of abduction too, huh? Why don't you say I hidden that kid Mandy away from you, huh?'

'OK, I will!' She managed to pull free of the black woman's grasp. 'I reckon that's exactly what you've done! You got her to give her perjured evidence and then you spirited her away before there could be any question of a retrial.'

'You are mad! Why should I do a crazy thing like that, huh?'

'Because, Madam Councillor, so long as Ari's inside that prison, he's your FAME meal ticket, that's why!'

The woman gasped, stepping back in shock before recovering enough to take a couple of wild swings at Kate. 'You—you lying, mad bitch!'

'Mandy was just another stunt, right! Oh, an inspired one. ITN was bound to go for it even if we didn't believe a single word. Brilliant! But never more than a stunt. Then, when my tame chief inspector showed up, you got panicky. Oh hell, how to stop that one?! So you staged that damned demo last night, knowing it would get him up on screen and into deep, deep trouble!'

Taff was still trying Kate's car-phone as Sergeant Warboys listed his way through the previous day's business: renewed responses to the Thames Valley crime figures, yet more racial problems in Wycombe, proposals for the Kidlington Open Day, another M4 pile up . . .

'Katie—at last! You OK?'

'Apart from having just endured a couple of rather bruising rounds with Councillor Edwards, yeah, baby, I'm just hunky. What can I do for you?'

'Any chance you could rush me down a copy of that Mandy Trotter tape you recorded?'

'Sure. How urgent?'

'Very.'

'Any point asking why?'

'Just a hunch, honey, just a hunch.'

'Give me an hour.'

Knowing her driving, Taff told her there wasn't that much of a hurry, then rang off.

'Now, Sergeant, what else?'

'Sir, with respect, Chief Superintendent Marsh was very—'

'Right then, phone his office to say I'm on the way.'

There was clearly little need for the phone call. Not only was the chief super's door wide open, the man stood framed in it like Rambo. Taff was barely inside before his boss let go with a growl.

'Not only off limits *again*, but messing with the bloody Edwards case!' Then, stomping off round his desk: 'Don't tell me! It's to do with your—your dear fiancée. Well obviously! That whole FAME nonsense! Honest to god, Roberts, how could you have let it happen? How *could* you!'

'They set me up, Guv'nor. Sorry.'

'Of course they set you up! Nothing could have been more obvious! But surely to God you could have foreseen the risk involved with a woman like Bella Edwards! Eh, man? Eh?'

Then, once again pre-empting Taff's reply: 'It's no good. Not this time. I honestly don't see how I can get you out of this one!'

'Er . . .'

'I've had his nibs on to me already. He's had Commander Hammond on requesting an explanation. You'll know, of course, it was Mr Hammond nailed Edwards.' He plumped down behind his desk, deeply perturbed. 'Just what the hell were you playing at? No, come on, tell me. I genuinely want to know. The facts now, not some bloody flannel.'

Taff did his best to explain about Mandy Trotter and thence to the assault on Kate. Chiefie Marsh, although his scowl deepened at the violence, was unimpressed by Taff's response.

'So you take that as a licence to go charging in gung-ho and to hell with standing orders, eh?'

'You couldn't have approved it for me, guv'nor.'

'That's for damn sure.'

'But as for just ignoring it—blow that.'

'Hm. Well, Roberts, that Welsh blood of yours could just have drowned you this time.' He gestured in evident distress. 'It's not as if this was just family. Whatever I report to the boss, he's going to have to pass it on to the Yard.'

'Sir, there is one possibility which, er, could provide the ideal response to Commander Hammond. It shouldn't take me more than an hour or so to confirm.'

The chief's scowl shifted to one of suspicion. 'I've had your Ideal Responses before, Roberts. Give me one good reason why I should indulge you on this one.'

'You—well, that is, sir, the Thames Valley force—we don't want egg on our faces, not if there's a good chance of avoiding it.' Then, heading off the man's retort: 'An hour and a half at the most, sir.'

'It had better be.' Marsh was already waving him out of the office. 'I can't hope to stall the governor much longer than that.'

Kate arrived at the press office so quickly that for a while it looked as if they'd easily meet Marsh's deadline. Before putting the Mandy video tape on to the screen, however, Taff poured Kate a strong coffee, then took her to where he had laid out several of the pathologist's mortuary photographs—those in fact showing the mutilated face of the murdered woman.

'Sorry about this, love, but is there any chance you might recognize this woman?'

Kate gasped, turning away to sink down into a chair and lower her head between her knees. 'Oh, Jees . . .'

'I'm sorry! I wouldn't have asked if it wasn't vital.' He turned to run the tape on the screen, freezing frame on Mandy's face. It didn't greatly help.

'You think this could be Mandy?' Kate whispered hoarsely, forcing herself back to the gruesome photographs.

'Do you?'

'I—oh my God . . . I've seen bodies before, but this . . .'

'How about the real thing?' Taff was already at the door to ask his secretary to get him the Royal Berks mortuary on the line. 'Take a look at the screen. There's a fancy little mole visible on her right cheek. I suppose you didn't notice if that was a stick-on job?'

'You're kidding. That went out with Marie Antoinette.'

'Right.' He broke off to speak on the phone to the mortuary, telling the assistant they would be along as soon as possible to view the victim.

Sergeant Warboys came fussing in as Taff snatched up the video and herded his ashen-faced fiancée out ahead of him. 'Hold the fort again, Tony, there's a good lad.'

Kate had consumed Taff's stock of sugar-mints and got some colour back into her cheeks by the time they reached the Royal Berks. Taff managed to park round the back near the mortuary, then introduced his girl to the pathologist who paused from his work to wave a pair of heavily-stained rubber gloves.

'Forgive my not shaking hands, Miss Lewis.' He gestured at the stiffs. 'Is this your first time?'

'She's none too used to mutilations.'

'Of course not. In fact I had Jim lay the lass out with that in mind.'

He led them past the ranked trolleys, each with its waxen cadaver awaiting examination. On a trolley at the top end near the mahogany doors of the refrigerated section was a shape with a white rubber sheet over it. The robust Jim stood waiting beside it poised like a grocer ready to display the goods. He gave Kate a big grin, holding his hands above and below his face to convey that he'd seen her on the TV screen. Then he leaned across to lift the rubber sheet away from the face with a showman's flourish. 'Turrah!'

But his macabre humour was lost on Kate, her eyes drawn compulsively to the tattered features.

'Oh, the poor soul . . .' The words came as little more than a gasp as she turned away. Yes, it resembled Mandy, but could she be sure? So much of recognition depended on personal animation—smile, gesture, voice tone, manner— that to see only the sunken, inanimate mask was altogether too remote. Was this really the tense, scratching young woman before the TV camera, the girl with the lisp and the odd catch in her voice? Was it the excited little hostess pouring them tea in the chintzy flat crammed with knick-knacks and cuddlies?

'Right,' Taff confirmed, holding tight to her hand, 'there's the mole, exactly where the video showed it. Of course, it wasn't visible in the forensic photos because of the, er, discolouration and . . .'

He broke off as Kate started to sob in pity, her hands to her face. 'To have died in such utter terror,' she whispered. 'The poor little girl—all alone.'

'I'm sorry, love, sorry.' Taff turned to the pathologist. 'At least we can now give you a positive identification on the victim. Named Miss Mandy Trotter and, prior to death, residing at a temporary address in Bayswater.'

'Well done, David.'

'We already knew she'd gone missing. The moment I saw your initial report about her being an attractive young black woman showing signs of a high level of sexual activity, I knew it was a possibility. Just a bit of luck the killer decided to dispose of her in our patch.'

'Lucky for you, Roberts? How do you figure that out?' Chiefie Marsh was no less suspicious now that CI Roberts had rushed back to his office with the news of the identification. 'Explain.'

'It gives me a legitimate reason, sir, for that visit to

Edwards in Wormwood Scrubs.' Then, in face of his chief's continuing scowl: 'It's a gruesome murder which we're naturally keen to clear up. Given the link between Mandy Trotter and the Edwards case, sir, there's every reason for a Thames Valley CI to have gone to the Scrubs and questioned Edwards.'

'Except . . .' The chief pulled a face, leaving the obvious disparity in the timing unstated. 'So what you're suggesting is that his nibs tells a bare-faced lie to Commander Hammond to the effect that last night you were officially assisting in the Marlbury murder investigation.'

Taff let a decent pause elapse before he built in the next bit. 'In point of fact, sir, it needn't be that much of a lie—not if I am actually attached to the case.' Then, racing on to make his point before Marsh could scoff it out the window: 'Apart from identifying the remains, sir, I've read through the entire trial transcript, I've got access to a video recording of the new evidence given to the PCA by the victim, I know where the deceased was domiciled, in fact I've examined her home, and . . .'

'All right, Roberts, no need to go into overkill.' He sat drumming his fingers in silence, the scowl unabated. 'You can be a cheeky bastard, I'll say that.'

'Only when my back's to the wall, sir.'

'Oh, it's that all right, no question.' There was another heavy pause, Ralph Marsh continuing to scowl while Taff Roberts sweated. 'Just how would you account for the fact that you visited Edwards *before* identifying the body?'

'Well, sir, one way might be for you simply to fail to mention that to the chief constable. Let him think I'd identified her before . . .'

'He's not a bloody simpleton, Roberts!'

'Exactly, sir, so he'll see what a handy face-saver it is—what a convenient way out of the problem.'

'*Your* problem!'

'Which none the less, guv'nor, would reflect on him.'

'God, man, you really do push your luck!'

Events took a dramatic turn in the Marlbury murder case today when Thames Valley police named the victim as 24-year-old society call-girl Mandy Trotter. Miss Trotter had recently recorded a statement with both ITN and the Police Complaints Authority claiming to have witnessed the killing seven years ago of prostitute Arlene Milton, for whose brutal murder a 40-year-old black man from Brixton, Aristotle Edwards, was gaoled for life in 1986.

Miss Trotter, pictured here recording her statement with ITN last month, insisted the man she saw brutally assaulting Arlene was white and in no way resembled Edwards for whom she had worked for more than a year. The video tape of her statement has been made available to the Thames Valley Police who have requested ITN not to air it in full until investigations have been taken further. Inevitably, however, there are suspicions that Mandy Trotter's murderer knew of her statement and had decided to silence her as a witness to the 1985 murder.

Rumours began last night that there had been developments in the notorious FAME campaign by Mrs Bella Edwards to win a retrial for her husband. This followed a visit by a senior police officer to question Aristotle Edwards in Wormwood Scrubs prison hospital where he is recovering from a near-fatal assault. ITN has now learnt that the officer, Chief Inspector David Roberts, until recently press officer for the Thames Valley force, has now joined the Thames Valley team investigating the death of Mandy Trotter.

The two Metropolitan Police officers responsible for convicting Edwards—Commander Edward Hammond and Superintendent Alec Barker, shown here at a press conference following the murder trial in 1986—were today unavailable for comment.

CHAPTER 10

'Lystons have an intriguing history,' Jack Walsh reported, 'somewhat akin to that of the Rake's Progress. Well back in the last century, the Lyston family diversified from landowners into property development. They rode the London property boom, building their power and wealth until, by the 1950s, they were solidly established in the City. By then, although property ownership was their core activity, they were also heavily into insurance and the brokering of commercial loans. Their success owed much to their reputation for straight dealing as a family concern.

'Then, by a chance of fate in the early 'seventies, Lystons took a radical turn. They completed a deal for a big slice of property in Mayfair which happened to include a defunct casino called Blandells. The place had lost its gaming licence a few years before, the owners had gone bankrupt and Blandells had stood unused and largely forgotten ever since. With, for them, uncharacteristic daring, the Board decided to restore the place and reapply for a licence. Being Lystons, they won ready support from the Betting Levy Board and took their first step into the gaming industry.

'Again fate intervened, this time in the form of sharp reverses in both the loan-brokering and insurance sides, forcing the sale of huge property holdings and obliging the company to rely increasingly on its fledgling venture into gaming. Such were the profit ratios, however, that in no time Lystons were expanding this side. Their past reputation for probity once again stood hugely to their advantage, enabling them to gain licences for betting-shops as well as launching new casinos, not only in London but also in Manchester, Glasgow and Newcastle.

'Of course, they encountered bitter resistance from rival gambling empires. Not just the full range of tricks in opposition to licence applications, but also the seedier ploys: threats of violence, anonymous vandalism and even the odd fire-bombing. By then, however, the company was too dependent on its gambling revenues to let itself be scared off.

'Predictably, the rivalry and threats intensified, rising to crisis pitch during the early 'eighties, by which time they virtually depended on their gambling interests. Hence, with the survival of its whole casino side at stake, the Board took a desperate decision. They voted to sell a large portion of Lystons private stock to Hammerville Inc., the Chicago hotel and entertainments empire. It was a marriage which brought them a crucial injection of muscle as well as money, promptly turning the tide on their rival gambling concerns.

'Every year since then, Lystons' published accounts have shown astronomical leaps, both in profits and assets. Undoubtedly, as well as the imported muscle, they also hire the smartest lawyers money can buy.'

'There's been a rush of calls from, well, er, angry old tarts. The editor asked me to handle them for you.'

'Exciting for you, Harley.' Kate eyed the young researcher with exaggerated disfavour: a typically naïve college graduate with a One-One in Media Studies and the initiative of a fresher. 'How'd you know they were angry?'

'Well, it's a predictable reaction to fear, Miss Lewis. They've all heard about Mandy Trotter's murder and that's scared them—hence all these calls to ITN wanting to know what's what. Some are asking if there's anything they can do. One or two are saying they'd seen Mandy around with various men and so on.'

'And you're checking them out, Harley? All these angry old tarts?' Then, at his half-nod: 'How? Meeting them, getting their details and pictures? If one of them happens to turn up dead, Mr Cawley's going to expect chapter and verse.'

'Of course.' To her surprise, he pulled out a file with half a dozen fact-sheets and pictures. 'Odd it should be the older ones. I'd have expected them to be less hysteria-prone.'

'Maybe the more years of service they put in, the more they realize how vulnerable they are.'

'Ah, I see.' He nodded politely, then pointed to one name on his list with a query against it. 'This one was slightly different. Most of them, for all their anger, obviously fancied their chances of getting on screen.'

'Handy publicity, eh. *A night of bliss with Dolly Smith as seen on Television!*'

'Right. Except this one took fright the moment I said to meet. She said she knew all about the original Edwards trial and knew about the real people behind it—the ones, she said, who'd murdered poor Arlene and now little Mandy as well. But she insisted there was no chance of her ever giving evidence.'

'Did you get a name?'

'No. Well, only a first name.' He pointed to the list. 'Janine.' He paused, blinking at the sharpness of Kate's response. 'What's wrong?'

'Harley, if this is Janine McKane and if she rings again —they do sometimes, you know, no matter how scared and nervous—do *anything* to reassure her and set up a meeting. Me and her—anywhere she specifies, any time, any place —just be sure and set it up.'

'Henry—at last! I was looking for you at the Three Hammers.'

'That's why I'm not there.' Henry was an old sweat with the Stepney CID who normally enjoyed a fruitful relationship with Jack Walsh but who right now was wishing he'd gone to the station canteen for his lunch. 'Do us a favour, will you, guv'nor.'

'All the other favours I've done you and you treat me like a leper?'

'You chose the right word there.' The detective-sergeant glanced uneasily around the bar, then nudged Walsh towards an alcove. 'What you're up to, guv'nor, you can't expect to rate in the popularity polls. I mean, why bloody Aristotle Edwards? I don't mind giving a hand when we're both on the same side. To be honest, I'm glad of the dosh. But don't come asking me to unstitch an evil villain like him.'

It surprised Walsh that word had reached a mere divisional sergeant. 'I wouldn't usually, you know that. In the normal course of events, you wouldn't find me anywhere near a case like this.'

'But?' The sergeant chuckled, pointing in irony. 'Don't tell me Bella the FAME got something on you. I have to admit to fancying some of those athletic kids of hers who leap off bridges in nothing but a harness, but somehow I'd never have thought that was your style.'

'No, you're right about that, Henry.' Walsh was in some difficulty himself over the credibility of this one. 'The thing is, the two coppers behind all this are playing far more dirty than just dropping the shutters on old Foxy Walsh. Take it from me, mate, they're way out of order.'

'Hey now, you're not going to tell me they're behind the death of that tom, Mandy whatsit.'

'That's how it looks.'

'No.' The sergeant shook his head, deeply reluctant to believe it. 'This is very high brass we're talking about. Yard gaffers.'

'Which must surely make you wonder how come they're bothering to put the word out all the way to a divisional sergeant like you.'

The detective scowled but offered no comment other than a slight shrug.

'I'll tell you: it's because Stepney happens to be home to a certain thieving snout whose name will not be a million mega-bytes away from your brain at this precise moment. Why? Because he's the snout who helped them fit up Edwards when he was on remand and who, because of that, they are particularly anxious to keep incognito.'

Another pause, the detective's face still dour and stubborn.

'If I'm wrong, old lad, if it wasn't a fit-up, why else do you suppose they'd bother sending the word down the line to you?' Pause. 'I did hear it right, didn't I? Alfie Small is a grass of yours.'

The sergeant sighed deeply, finally yielding. 'You can be very persuasive, Mr Walsh.'

'I wish to God it didn't have to be this one. Senior Yard brass, like you say, and all for a lousy black pimp who likely deserves a life-sentence for all the other shitty jobs he's pulled, if not for doing in Arlene Milton.' He paused as Henry scribbled him a note, then glanced at it. 'What's this?'

'A club in Southend where he's been working as a barman. If Alf don't show up, bell me and I'll tell you where else to look. Get your fancy boyfriend along there this evening about eight.'

'My . . . ?'

'It's obvious you ain't in this alone, guv'nor. If it was you on your own, you'd never be after them like this. Never. The number of cases you fitted up with a bit of extra to be sure and swing the verdict when you knew you'd got the right villain. No, no, you'd be more tolerant than that Welsh git.'

'The day I start worrying about what some Stepney CID sweat thinks about me, I'll—I'll apply for a transfer to the Orkneys.' Taff grimaced in dismissal. Yet he and Papa Walsh both knew it wasn't true. Even a Welsh maverick doesn't commit himself to a force which depends on a high level of mutual trust and esprit de corps without caring what his team mates think of him. Only snooty types like Commander Hammond affected indifference, and then it was only a front.

'Anyway, if he disapproves so much, why's he helping out?'

Walsh shrugged. He had asked himself the same question. The most rational answer seemed to be that at heart Henry cared more for the integrity of the force than he chose to let on, also that there were definite limits to misconduct beyond which officers of whatever rank must be stopped from going. But there was also the more human explanation of loyalty to an erstwhile guv'nor whose judgement Henry respected, however foxy he might have been as a serving officer at the Yard.

Of course there was also the squalid alternative that the sergeant was reluctant to give Walsh a flat rejection and had hence sent them on a wild-goose chase.

Indeed, it was rather beginning to look that way. They had been over an hour in the Southend club already and still no sign of Alfred Small. The place was a rather dubious 'health club' with gymnasium, sauna, billiards and two bars, also a lounge section frequented by chicks ready to cater for the aftermath of a work-out or massage. The management had been more than happy to sign them in on a temporary-membership basis to have a few drinks while they considered joining.

The question was whether Alf simply hadn't yet arrived for work or else was occupied out of sight somewhere like the kitchens or, worse, whether they had failed to recognize him from the CRO picture supplied by Harvey Bolt.

'My money goes on the tall waiter with the tash,' Walsh remarked at last. 'This mugshot dates from his last remand six years ago. Since then he could well have thinned out on top, got fatter and flabbier. As for the whiskers, he could easily have grown those since dropping out of sight. Take a good look—it's got to be him.'

'Agreed,' Taff murmured, 'and I'll tell you something else: Barker, or whoever sent him down here, warned him to be careful and watch out for company. And right now he's clocked that we're interested in him.' He drained his beer, stood up and sauntered off towards the gents.

The toilets opened off a passageway at the end of which was a fire-exit door opening out into the car park. Taff made it outside and headed round to a yard at the back behind the kitchens just in time to glimpse the waiter fumbling to unlock the door of an old Ford Cortina. The copper shouted out and sprinted forward, panicking the man away from the car and off towards an alleyway at the far corner. Then, pausing only to heave a tall cylindrical waste-bin across the mouth of the alley, he took off.

Taff hit the bin at full speed, trying to vault over it, only to feel it topple under his weight. He went sprawling, his feet slipping in a mess of vegetable peelings as he struggled to resume the chase. Flabby or not, Alf Small was now hoofing it like a good 'un. Fortunately, the alleyway led to an area of open parkland, so that Taff was able to glimpse his quarry at the further side as Small dived between rows of garages behind a block of flats. Before the Welshman

was even half way across the park, however, a couple of
marauding dogs joined in, barking as they raced up, the
one snapping at Taff's ankles with such determination that
he tripped and went a purler into a flowerbed.

The two dogs escorted him in noisy excitement as he
hobbled the remaining few yards to the garages. He
searched around a bit but could find no sign of the fugitive.
Bruised, filthy and too badly winded even to swear, he gave
up.

The dogs stayed with him, commenting loudly as he
limped back across the park. The smaller of the two, a
modified Jack Russell, definitely deserved the muzzle-of-
the-year award. Not until they encountered the overturned
dustbin in the alleyway did the pair relinquish their Southend hospitality in search of scraps.

Small's Cortina was still parked behind the kitchens. To
Taff's surprise, as he headed for the car park, he noticed
there was someone in it—two men, in fact, seated in the
front. He crouched down, lunging sideways behind another
bin, only to grin as a familiar voice called across.

'Hey, boyo, come on and meet Mr Snout.'

'Like old times,' Taff grunted, limping across to climb
into the back of the Cortina. 'I do the legwork, you get the
collar.'

'Quite right and proper, my son.'

It was some satisfaction to Taff to see that Alf Small was
also severely winded and gasping in pain with every breath.
'Got a fag, guv?'

'Stick of gum's the best I can manage.' Walsh handed
him one. 'Police officers are healthy people, as you'll just
have observed. Capable of the four-minute mile, regulars
in the London Marathon. This, however, is not last year's
winner but an officer with the Thames Valley force, who
are generally less noted for their athletic prowess than the
lads of the Met.'

'Name of Roberts,' the fugitive panted. 'Right?'

'Where'd you get that idea?'

'A certain gentleman of the Yard.' He turned to Taff.

'He said if you came pestering me I was to give you a message. He said to tell you to watch out it doesn't snow on you. Snow, right? Whatever that means.'

'It's a threat,' Taff remarked. 'As it happens, an empty and meaningless threat. But Superintendent Barker doesn't know that. He thinks he's got an edge on me—a means of blackmailing me—just the same as he has on you. But as it happens he's wrong on both counts. Because what he's got on you becomes totally worthless the moment Barker is discredited. And the key to that, Mr Small, rests with *you*. Savvy?'

The snout was twisted awkwardly round in the front seat, staring in shock as Taff continued, his voice flat and remorseless. The enforcer, Walsh thought as he listened to the younger officer. This is no job he's in, this is a vocation. The money, the pension rights, the status, they're all irrelevant. Once perhaps, when he first came to me, but not any longer. This boy's driven by an altogether different engine now. Maybe it's the vengeance aspect after what they tried on with his Katie. Maybe it's that simple. But no, like hell it is. That was just the excuse he needed to get mounted up and come thundering in at the charge.

'Why do you think Barker was so anxious to hide you away?' Taff persisted. 'He had to put the fear into you and get you well away from your usual haunts because he knows you're the weak link.'

Small's expression confirmed that he certainly had had the fear put into him, and very convincingly, too. 'Please, guv,' he stammered, 'lay off, will you.'

'You're the key, Alf. Come clean about Ari Edwards's so-called prison-yard confession, testify that it was Alec Barker who put you up to it, then he goes down and you're off the hook. Easy.'

'You must think I'm a complete and utter dick-head!'

'On the contrary, I think it'll be a release—an enormous weight off your back.'

'Chief, you can do what you bloody like, but there is no

way on God's earth you'll ever get me giving evidence in court.'

'I'll guarantee you immunity from prosecution . . .'

'Yeah? What about the grave and all while you're at it?' Then, persisting over the combined responses of both Taff and Walsh: 'No courtrooms, and that's flat.'

'All right,' Taff cracked back, 'it's a deal. No court, but you record a confession on camera, during which you state that the tape is not to be used as court evidence.'

This time it was Walsh who objected, playing Box and Cox as he urged the chief inspector not to throw it away with such an absurd concession. But Taff explained that he could fully understand Alf's dread of court exposure. The snout had his future to think of, after all. A tape-recorded confession was the most they could reasonably expect of him. And, no, of course it wouldn't be a police recording. On the contrary, the whole procedure could be done totally away from the police, in fact at the ITN studios.

'Think of it as an insurance, Alf,' he told the terrified snout as he got out of the Cortina prior to telephoning Kate on his car-phone. 'Think of it as an investment in the future.'

Taff telephoned Kate from the club, arranging for her to have a studio ready. To his huge alarm, however, when he returned to the club's kitchen yard he found the Cortina empty. Desperately, he started searching around, only to react at renewed barking from the alleyway followed by muffled groans and a wheezing call for help.

At first, recognizing the retired chiefie among the garbage, Taff thought the snout had downed him and fled. But then, to his huge relief, he realized Walsh was on top of the slippery Alf whose face he was pressing firmly into the spilled slops with noisy encouragement from the two dogs.

'Pedigree Chummy here got camera shy,' Walsh explained, clambering free with relief as Taff hoisted the groaning snout clear of dogs and garbage and frog-marched

him away to the car park. 'Luckily some of us can turn on
a touch of speed when it counts.'

'Liar,' Alf muttered. 'I'd have been way out of sight but
for them damn dogs.'

On the drive back to London, with prompting from Taff
and Walsh, the snout grudgingly revealed the process which
had led to his appearance as one of the Crown's prime
witnesses in the Aristotle Edwards murder trial. In the first
instance, he had been put heavily on the spot by a Stepney
detective-sergeant, in fact Henry's predecessor. The deal
was that unless Alf agreed to go on remand and grass up
the black pimp, he'd find himself stitched up so tightly he'd
pull a minimum ten-year stretch; conversely, if he agreed
to do it, he could look forward to a trouble-free run for as
long as the DS remained on Stepney CID. As the DS had
pointed out at the time, it was one of those deals Alfie
simply couldn't refuse.

No, he had never dealt with anyone other than the DS,
although it was obvious to him that at the very least DCI
Barker must be behind it, possibly Hammond as well. However, it was the DS who had collared Alf on a trumped-up
burglary charge, duly landing him in custody on remand
in Brixton prison. Once inside, Alf had started cultivating
a friendship with the black American pimp, spending as
much time in his company as possible. Then, after a couple
of weeks, he had gone and reported to one of the assistant
governors that Ari had confessed to him about the murder.

There had ensued a couple of heavy interviews with
Barker, during which the then DCI had effectively told him
what to state and then sign to in his statement, duly giving
him a copy and telling him to be sure and memorize every
detail ready for the trial when he could certainly expect to
face tough cross-examination. In the event, that ordeal had
proved less daunting than expected, Edwards's defence
generally proving somewhat limp by comparison with the
Crown's robust prosecution.

Well before the trial, however, indeed at the first remand
hearing after signing the so-called confession statement, Alf

was freed from prison. Taken to the magistrates' court, he heard the prosecutor say that, after reviewing the evidence, the Crown was withdrawing its objections to bail. Alf's actual trial on those charges was then adjourned several times, in fact until shortly after he had testified in the Old Bailey about Ari's non-existent confession. Less than a month later, at Alf's next court appearance on the burglary charges, the prosecutor announced that, following ammendments to crucial parts of the police evidence, the CPS had been obliged yet again to review this long-drawn-out affair and had concluded the case against Mr Small was now altogether too weak to justify a trial; accordingly, albeit with some misgiving, the Crown was asking the bench to dismiss the case. This the stipendiary magistrate duly did, along with some crisp comments about police ineptitude and costs awarded to Mr Small.

'Just an everyday story of Met manipulation,' Taff muttered curtly to Walsh, 'unwittingly aided and abetted by the Crown Prosecution Service.'

'What really had me gob-smacked,' Alf added, 'was that a week later I'm taking a drink down the boozer when this natty-looking geezer trots up and stuffs an envelope into my pocket. Inside I find a grand in tenners and a note telling me it's to make up for the inconvenience of my stay in Brixton. Now there's no way that came from Brother Barker. Which means there's got to be someone looking over his shoulder, right. And that, my friends, is why there's no possible way I can go public with any retraction. Record this tape and use it to put the frighteners on Barker, fair enough. But nothing else or—or Alfie Small's going to end up as stiff as that tart Trotter.'

The elation had gone out of it for Taff. Going after Barker as the chief perpetrator had been fair game: focus on the target and go for it with the sharp clarity of vengeance. But to have it confirmed that Barker was no less a pawn in the game than Alf Small, oh dear, dear! Some small relief, perhaps, to learn that Barker wasn't a copper turned killer.

But to have the parameters of the investigation now shift to embrace the vast and impersonal might of Lystons plc and the sinister mobsters behind them . . .

Kate on the other hand was cock-a-hoop. As they finished the video taping she darted forward and, to his sweaty confusion, hugged the awful snout. 'Brilliant! Six years of the FAME campaign, which Councillor Edwards manipulated to her own selfish ends and which she never wanted to succeed. Now, despite her efforts, we've drawn blood!'

'Don't over-rate it,' Taff warned her later after they'd dropped off first Walsh and then Alf at the station for a train to Southend. 'It's handy as a bargaining chip,' yes, but not much else.' Then, over-riding her retort: 'So we got the snout to change his tune and one of the prosecution planks collapsed. But it was never the main plank. And since he's anyway refusing to testify under oath in court —' he shrugged—'it remains to be seen just how far we've really advanced.'

Taff was to get the first vibes on that within the hour. They hadn't been home very long, were still playing back the Ansafone tape, when a live call came through.

'Roberts, it's Barker. It's about time we met about the Edwards case.'

Taff had to admire Barker's choice of venue. There was no way he was going to risk Taff's carrying a body microphone or else being recorded on a long-range directional mike. So he specified that they met at the Westminster Swim Centre, in the shallow end of the subsidiary pool.

'Is this venue pure expediency or are you a regular swimmer?'

'I try to keep fit, Roberts.'

Not with much success, Taff thought. But then, at least with the long-distance practitioners, body fat could be an asset. Nor, for that matter, did the man look unduly tense; but appearances could also be deceptive, even when clad only in a bathing costume.

'So you got to Small.' From the casualness of his tone,

he might have been remarking on the water temperature.
'For what that's worth.'

'Enough to force a retrial,' Taff bluffed, wondering
whether Barker had heard it from Alf himself and if not
from whom. 'More than enough, in fact, when taken in
conjunction with the murder of Mandy Trotter.'

'Ah. Poor Miss Trotter. Well we'd hardly be paddling
here now but for her.'

'And also that gross bloody assault on Kate.'

'Miss Lewis?' He stared in concern, shaking his head. If
he already knew, Taff thought, he was pretty smart at hiding it. 'What assault?'

Taff told him, in fact augmenting it by claiming she'd
suffered the full rape before managing to fight free. He was
watching the man for the slightest give-away, but there was
none. Barker appeared genuinely shocked, finally plunging
off to swim a couple of lengths before responding.

'No doubt it sounds improbable to you that I had no
idea, much less any control over such a dreadful thing, but
that's the fact of it. No more, believe me, than I had over
the murder of that poor wretched girl Trotter.'

'You going to tell me it was Hammond and not you?'

'Hammond!' He shook his head in rejection. 'An admin-
istrator. Brilliant with computers, but as for crime—"leave
the sleuthing to you, Alec."' He flopped back in the
water, briefly sinking below the surface in almost symbolic
immersion.

'So who did kill Mandy Trotter?' Taff asked when he
surfaced. 'You must know.'

'If I did, believe me, I'd tell you. Murder. Of course I
would.' Then, wagging his head over it, he added: 'For my
money, the most probable person to help you with that is
Ari Edwards.'

'Oh, come on, what about the people behind you?' Then,
when the Met super merely wiped the water from his face
and blinked at him: 'The big boys looking over your shoulder, that's how Alf put it. The ones who slipped Alf a
thousand pounds in return for his perjury and his three

weeks on remand in Brixton. What about them? What about Lystons?'

The effect was galvanic. Hitherto, apart from his show of concern over the assault on Kate, Barker had appeared totally in command of the situation. Not any more. He stood up, water draining from his slack white flesh as he lunged forward to grip Taff's arm. 'You want another death? Mine and—and likely Alf Small's as well? Because damn sure they'd see me off in short order if I so much as breathed a whisper to you about them!'

'There comes a time,' Taff snapped, jerking back, 'when the scales come to outweigh the risk.'

'What do you mean?'

'So far you've got Mandy's death, Kate's rape and more than six years of Ari Edwards's life all weighing on the one side. How much more are you going to load on through dread of the Mob's bloody vengeance?'

'His freedom,' Barker blurted in desperation, 'I'll get Edwards his freedom! That's something on the positive side. Not a lot, I admit. We can't undo the girl's death or —or the rape, damn it. But at least . . .'

'The name of your original informant.'

'What?'

'The one who first put you on to Edwards. Name him and you've got yourself a deal.'

'And a death warrant!' He was backing away, shaking his head, his hands slapping at the water. 'Please, Roberts, you must see the two are linked. He's one of Lystons' men. So they're both equally taboo!' He backed inadvertently into a passing swimmer, thrusting the startled girl sharply aside before repeating the plea. 'Please, Roberts!'

Taff thought it over, weighing the situation like a torts lawyer haggling over an injury. The Alf Small video tape was indeed of little use as real evidence, a fact of which Barker seemed well aware. There appeared to be no chance of forcing him to name the original informant or giving evidence against Lystons. At the end of it all, the best prospect seemed acceptance of his offer to get Aristotle Edwards out of prison. Just how he would achieve that, Taff could only guess. But as the two investigating officers, Barker and Hammond were the ones best placed to initiate the reversal process and get him freed.

'You get that toady CI of yours in records to scrap the investigation of Jack Walsh and get all his gear back to Klein Holdings. Right?'

'And?'

'You and Hammond do whatever has to be done to get Ari Edwards released—without a retrial.'

CHAPTER 11

'You were blinded by your own damned ambition, Ted. So red hot for a spectacular conviction to boost your promotion that you left it all to old Alec. No need to double-check anything, just send it through on the nod; but make good and sure you grab the bulk of the credit.'

Barker had managed to get the commander well away from the Yard for lunch at Wheelers, aware that telling it all to him, over oysters and Chablis would deflect too loud a response. In fact, Hammond must have anticipated something of what his erstwhile number two was going to say since he was taking it for the most part in glum silence, challenging little, failing even to rise to the jibe about his excessive ambition. Indeed, in an odd way, it was something of a relief to him.

The fact was, no matter how fickle and gimmicky all those endless FAME stunts over the years, they'd had a cumulative impact way across Hammond's stress threshold. That plaguing black opportunist wife of a pimp, using her husband's brutal crime to clamber up the dunghill of her own sordid political ambitions—and in the process imputing racial prejudice on the part of the CID officers handling the case. No matter how solid the evidence against Edwards, the mere vigour and persistence of her

FAME protests meant that some mud had inevitably stuck over the years . . . to the point where eventually, when the Trotter tart had emerged with her so-called new evidence, he'd found himself wishing to God the whole thing could simply terminate once and for all.

'What are you saying, Alec? Just what is it that's changed?'

'Number one is that blessed prison-yard confession. The way it looks, Alfie Small's been nobbled by the media. They've offered him a fat fee to change his tune. The word is, if we don't act fast, they'll have him on *Rough Justice* saying I put the screws on him to lie about that whole confession.'

'Did you?'

'You've got to be kidding! Apart from anything else, guv'nor, we had such a strong case against Edwards, there was no need. The snag is, what with all this endless pressure for retrials since PACE—all the IRA bombers, the Bridgwater three, Winston Silcot and all the bloody rest—any formal retraction by Small would be bound to force a full review of the case. Moreover, under PACE rules, we'd also lose the whole of Edwards's interrogation confession. Add to that the posthumous video testimony of the Trotter girl and I reckon we'd be on very weak ground indeed.'

To Barker's surprise and relief, the commander merely nodded in dour agreement. 'So what are you suggesting?'

'Go to the DPP. Make the points about Small, about PACE and also Mandy Trotter, then suggest they either go for a retrial and offer no evidence or, if the Director thinks she can swing it with Lord Justice Streeter, get the appeal court to quash it.'

'And the bastard walks free!'

'Seven years he's done in all. The equivalent of over fifteen with remission.'

'Damn you!' the senior officer hissed, leaning close to hide his surge of frustration and guilt. 'You were the one who was so cocksure of everything! You were the man from Vice who knew the whole tom trade inside out—picking up whispers left, right and centre—telling me there was no doubt whatsoever—solid as a rock, guv'nor, don't you fret. So what the hell was I supposed to do?'

Barker sat back to drink wine and let the senior officer cool down. He could well have retorted that Hammond had acted irresponsibly, abdicating his supervision of the case and disregarding the command structure in his hunger for glory. Yet there was nothing to gain from further recriminations.

'Look, guv'nor, what we're into now is a damage-limitation exercise.' Then, persisting over the commander's snort: 'Just play it all honourable, why not? Take advantage of the reverses over the IRA bombers and the rest. Remind the DPP what an earnest crusader for truth you are, then point out to her that, what with the new standards of proof brought in under PACE, you reckon it's high time the Edwards case was reviewed.'

'You made your point, damn it. No need to be facetious as well.'

'Guv'nor, I'm simply suggesting a line for the DPP, bearing in mind the Director's then got to sell it to the appeal judges. Like I said, we're into damage limitation, you and me both. The one thing we've *got* to avoid is anyone ordering an internal inquiry.'

'God forbid!'

'Exactly. OK, we both know there'll be Leftie MPs yelling for blood. But there's no way they'll get anywhere unless the judiciary say so.' He paused at Hammond's persisting scowl, then added: 'Listen, as well as giving the DPP the crusader-for-truth bit, warn her about the Cabinet Bimbo angle. Point out how that hidden camera didn't *just* take those pictures of Arlene Milton and Janine McKane. Its main function was to take pictures of Arlene Milton with her clients. Tell him, if the defence renew their attempts to get these notorious clients to give evidence, oh dear, dear, could be a lot of egg on a lot of Establishment faces.' He snorted in irony. 'If honour doesn't sway him, damn sure dishonour will.'

*

The statement read out by the senior appeal court judge, Lord Justice Streeter, stated that the court had reviewed all the evidence from the original trial in conjunction with new evidence which has recently come to light. After close consideration, the appeal judges had concluded there were, as of now, insufficient grounds to sustain the original verdict of guilt recorded by the jury against Aristotle Edwards in his trial in 1986 for the murder of Arlene Milton.

Lord Justice Streeter concluded: Because, in agreement with my two fellow appeal judges, I consider that a retrial would not serve the interests of justice, the life sentence on Aristotle Edwards is quashed forthwith.

There was a burst of wild cheers and chanting from the crowds of FAME supporters, Randi Dubois and Bella parading in front of the television cameras with their hands raised like a couple of triumphant Wimbledon stars. Meanwhile, hard-headed professional that she was, Kate swallowed her cynicism, put on a smile and started forward through the crowd to interview the exultant couple.

This is the scene outside the FAME community centre following the official announcement from the Appeal Court, the massed supporters of the Free Aristotle Macho Edwards campaign proclaiming victory for the man for whose freedom they have campaigned with such relentless vigour over the last six years. Already the carnival spirit is taking hold and preparations beginning for one of Brixton's biggest ever street parties.

And here are the two people to whom Ari Edwards most owes his forthcoming freedom: his wife Bella, who over six years of tireless compaigning has staged numerous demos and stunts to publicize the cause, in the process raising hundreds of thousands of pounds, mainly from Brixton's black community. In addition, she has obtained substantial grants for the conversion of a local warehouse into the FAME Community Centre and has twice been elected a Labour councillor.

'Mrs Edwards, today's announcement is a huge triumph for your perseverance and devotion to the cause of your husband's freedom.'

'Thank you, M'am, thank you! And you media folk sure done

your bit, what with all that terrific coverage you gave us over the years.'

'Years, Councillor, during which you have built up this substantial organization—the community centre, thousands of supporters, the core of up to a dozen young FAME teamsters. But what of the future? Now that you have achieved such spectacular success, will that simply mean the end of FAME? Or might you perhaps channel the enormous energies and talents of your team into other black causes?'

'I guess you're right, M'am. A family of brothers and sisters like ours is too special simply to let it fall apart with the birth of that one big event we all been struggling for over so long. And, let me tell you, the fact that it's taken us all these years to get any action just goes to show what deep-rooted racist attitudes we all up against. When black people raise their voices in protest like we did, sure as hell the knee-jerk response of people in authority is to slam the door and close their ears. So yes, Miss Lewis, I guess the answer to your question is this: so long as there are black causes to fight, we should damn sure keep the FAME team together and fight them.'

'A formidable prospect.'

'OK, right. But I'll tell you this, baby, right now we aim to put all our energies and talents into one great helluva hooray!'

'Of which we might see something later.'

'You'd better all be there, kid.'

'Thank you, Bella Edwards. And now, turning to the legal muscle behind today's success: Mr Randi Dubois is a locally-based Brixton lawyer whose office off the Brixton Road is seldom likely to be short of clients after today's success. Mr Dubois, can you say just what aspect of the evidence you think most swayed the three appeal judges to this decision?'

'Well, Miss Lewis, taking all the reasons Lord Justice Streeter gave for their judgement, I guess the strongest answer coming through is the change in the ground rules for police interrogation introduced in the Police and Criminal Evidence Act. Same as it was with the Birmingham Six and the Guildford Bombers and all the other successful appeals like them. By changing the rules of interrogation, they made all those convictions unsafe. Why? Because under the new rules, there is no way His Honour Judge Willis could ever have allowed

the jury to hear about those two alleged confessions—the one to
Detective-Inspector Barker and also that wacky prison-yard fiction.
If you read through his lordship's judgement, they were both held to
be unsafe.

'So what does that leave against my man Ari? The suspect evidence
of a convicted prostitute who claimed she'd seen Ari carrying something to his car; also that whole phoney motive stuff of the mystery
girl Janine McKane, photographed at some unspecified time in company with Arlene Milton in the room where she died. So what?
Proves nothing. I mean, not to be disrespectful towards the appeal
judges, but they were on to a hiding to nothing. They simply had to
do what they've just done: avoid any retrial and just quash the
verdict.'

'So you're satisfied, Mr Dubois, that today justice has finally been
done?'

'Satisfied that it's started, Miss Lewis. It won't be fully done till
there's been an inquiry into how the original police investigation
could have led to such a monstrous injustice; also until we see what
compensation they're offering Ari for six years of wrongful imprisonment. Six of the prime years of his life, a nightmare time during
which he's received numerous assaults, both physical and mental, no
less than four periods of solitary confinement in the punishment block,
the total loss of his means of earning, no prospects of a job, his
previous life in tatters. That's the sum total of this miscarriage of
justice. So let's see what sort of compensation they're offering for all
that before we talk of justice.'

'Did Lord Justice Streeter's judgement include any recommen-
dations about compensation?'

'None. They copped out on that issue, same as they did over a
retrial. Frankly, we'd have welcomed a retrial because then we could
have given all the prosecution evidence a full airing and shown the
world how Ari Edwards is totally innocent and not one thing against
him. That's likely why the appeal judges didn't order it that way:
far cleaner for the legal establishment simply to cop out, quash it and
have done. But let me tell you this, the first advice I'm giving Ari when
he walks out that prison is to demand his right to full compensation.'

'Just how soon is he likely to be released? Have you had any
indication of that?'

*'That's not too much the Home Office style to rush these things.
But you can be sure there'll be a bunch of us heading down the prison
real soon to give him the reception he deserves the moment they open
those doors.'*

'Yes, Mr Barker, I did hear the news. I'm going to have
some very heavy questions coming down to me from
upstairs, so I hope you're calling me with some useful
answers.'

'Firstly, is this line safe?'

'Hundred per cent.'

'You certain?' Alec Barker was wetter almost than when
he'd met the remorseless CI Roberts in the pool, sweating
with anxiety, fear and self-loathing. All his troubles, every
damned one of them, had started with his transfer to Vice.
Before that, dealing with straightforward villainy, he had
been no more prone to temptation than he'd been aware
of his own weaknesses. Solidly married, kids at college,
everything straight and above board, everything to lose; the
idea of taking a bribe or of bending the rules had been
totally alien to him. Then had come Vice, and with it the
discovery of appetites and lusts as insistent as any
addiction.

Over forty years old, more than twenty years a copper,
yet sucked into the tender trap with the naïvety of a teen-
ager. And the deeper in, the more that addiction had taken
hold. Anything—*anything*—for the new experience, the
fresh trick. No matter that it was basically always the same
old lark along with the same sort of leggy lass. Always the
expectation, the raw lust, had drawn him back into it. And,
idiot that he was, he'd had absolutely no suspicions about
where he was being led until one day, quite suddenly, the
photographs, the threats, the obligations; the end of the
fun, the start of the pay-off.

And pay he had, ever since; and never more heavily than
with the Edwards conviction. *Cut all this hypocritical crap about
the guilty man going free, Barker; you'll get a famous conviction and
all the glory and promotion that goes with it.* Well, not any more!

'Tell your Lyston bosses, Alan—tell them I managed to arrange it so there was no retrial and no risk of the DPP ordering an internal inquiry. The Director simply went to the appeal judges and advised them to scrap the whole nonsense. He pointed out how the confession evidence was unsound and any retrial was going to leave everyone, especially His Honour Judge Willis, looking a royal prat, not to mention the risk of exposing a good few of Arlene's Establishment clients whose naughty photographs could yet come to light. Let Edwards out, he told the judges, and have done.'

'Very clever of you, Alec, I'm sure. But as you well know, our problems start with the last bit.'

'Sorry?'

'Why let him out? What the bloody hell?'

'There were problems. The stitching was coming undone.'

'So why not let Terry Whittal deal with it in the obvious way? There's no shortage of hit men in stir.'

'Now listen,' the superintendent snapped, 'there's been more than enough blood already! When I tipped you off about the statement from that Trotter girl, the last thing on earth I reckoned was—was a brutal killing like that!'

'Is that so? Well then, Alec my old son, you were a bit of a stupid innocent, weren't you!'

The phrase caught Barker off balance, echoing all too closely the one he had used at the Wheelers' lunch to rebuke Commander Hammond. 'Blinded by your own damned ambition, Ted!'

Yes, here he comes at last—receiving, as you can see, a tumultuous welcome. Surely, whatever one may feel about the justice of this man's release, Ari Edwards is already well on the way to folk-hero status. Already there have been two hit songs popularized by the FAME team on the Free-Ari theme. Whatever the future may hold for the man, the saga of his wife's struggle to win him justice must lodge in the annals of legend as well as in the Guinness Book of Records.

Kate paused, wondering ruefully how much of this whole bizarre circus would be edited out. No doubt, knowing Bella's usual luck, they'd hit a low-news night and end up making the blessed lead! Certainly, given ITN's exclusive possession of the Mandy Trotter tape, Lawrence would want to run it pretty big. Another Kate Lewis scoop! Yet, as so often, there was that sour taste behind it. The real truth was, as usual, very different from the glitzy version they'd be putting out on the screen. The terse judgement issued by the appeal court, for instance, obviously gave no hint of Barker's guilt over manufacturing the prison-yard confession. Likewise, Taff's hand in forcing the issue had to be tactfully excluded. At the end of the day, the credit had to go to Randi and Bella and to hell with the full story.

To Kate's surprise, the triumph displayed by his FAME supporters was not echoed by the player at the centre of the drama. Maybe it was pain from his injuries, still not fully healed after a couple of months to judge from his awkward limp and the sling supporting his arm, or maybe it was the impact of freedom on a man so long imprisoned. Whatever, there was little hint of elation in Ari's face as he raised his clenched fist in response to the burst of cheers and chanting.

Kate was close enough, too, to sense the falseness of his smile for buxom Bella as she hugged and kissed him, also to see the wince of pain as the reunited pair were hoisted shoulder-high for the triumphal parade around the Scrubs forecourt. Certainly there was none of the ebullience and fun with which the man had swaggered across the prison visiting hall to greet her and Randi. Nor could he manage much in the way of fizz when he finally escaped the FAME athletes to give Kate a few words in front of the camera. What he did manage was to whip his good arm around her and jerk her close for a kiss—something which, given the nature of his prior trade, she could well have done without —yet equally, something which her bastard of an editor would never agree to cut.

'Welcome to freedom, Mr Edwards. In a word, how does it feel?'

'One word ain't enough, honey. But one message I gotta shout loud and clear: Thank you, Chief Inspector David Roberts for being the one honest cop in this whole mother-fucking country!'

'And thank God for tape editing,' Kate cracked back at him, 'because there is no way the editor can let *that* go out on *News at Ten!*'

The street party might well have been Brixton's biggest ever had it not come on to rain with test-match determination, soaking the improvised floats and hi-camp costumes, and driving the rap and reggae bands, the massed dancers and the loaded refreshment tables, away into the shelter of the community centre.

Kate was secretly relieved. It was a pity, of course, to see the display of Caribbean jubilation briefly dampened, not least since the vast majority of the participants fully deserved a good knees-up; years of eager support and a great deal of hard-earned cash donated towards the freedom of a man most of them had never met, yet whom the force of Bella's publicity machine had elevated to the status of folk hero.

So why Kate's sense of relief? She wasn't entirely sure. Perhaps to do with the volumes of hash and strong liquor and even stronger drugs like crack, all freely available? Or was it something deeper and less cerebral stirring at the core of her nature? A rising sense of abandon, spurred by her own body chemistry in response to the relentless rhythm of the music and the aura of massed euphoria that was Carnival. For, well-bred WASP celebrity that she was, it made her deeply uneasy to feel she could be slithering steadily towards an abyss of total abandon.

The deafening scene inside the community hall resembled a cross between Hieronymus Bosch's vision of hell and a student-rag attempt to cram the maximum number of bods into the smallest possible space. Leaving the ITN team near the main entrance, Kate wriggled her way through the pulsing mob towards the office. It cost her a couple minutes and several goosings to get there. But once there it was like stepping into an oasis—of space, if not of silence. Whereas nothing could have shut out the throbbing roar of amplified reggae from the main hall, there was a lot of excitement in the office itself thanks to the improvised telephone auction. With Bella on one phone, Leena on another and Winston on a mobile, the three were juggling contact with a variety of Sunday newspapers while Randi Dubois dashed from one to the other vigorously talking up the price of Ari's story: 'Full serialization? Over how long?'—'Exclusive world-wide is a whole lot bigger than exclusive UK—likewise the screen rights.'—'Explicit, frank and unabridged, baby! You gotta believe it.'—'Syndication? OK, but that's gotta cost you pro rata on the number of outlets.'—'Hey now, sir, if you want the Bimbo angle, you're into the mega-bucks league.'

Meanwhile, sitting back with his feet up on the desk as he puffed at a slim cigar and sipped Buck's fizz, the liberated Ari Edwards seemed unconscious of the surging hysteria which greeted each hike in the price of his secrets, actual or ghosted, true or legend.

He became visibly more animated at sight of Kate, raising her a wry grin when she asked how he could possibly be so casual after years of earning less than 50p a day in prison. But he offered no reply other than to make another grab at her—a move which this time she was quick to dodge.

Before long, however, she realized that, behind the hooded eyelids and show of listless disinterest, the black man was in fact keenly monitoring each incoming call. In the event, the one he was waiting for came in on Leena's line.

'Hello, FAME office, who's this? . . . What, personal? Speak up, OK . . . Depends who wants him . . . Hang on.' She covered the phone. 'Some whisperer here says he wants to give you a message, Ari.'

'He say a name?'

'Sounded like Jerry—Perry, Terry—whatever.'

In two strides, the big blackman was across to take the phone from her. 'Here's the man. What's the message?'

He listened expressionless for a few moments, then grunted and handed the receiver back to Leena to hang up.

'So who was it?'

Ari shrugged, shaking his head in rejection. 'Some Holy Joker calling on me to renounce sin and be born again.'

'You kidding? Hey, man, where you going?'

'To take a leak instead.' It was said casually, the man taking his ebony stick to hobble to the side door where he paused to leer teasingly back at Kate. 'You want to come along, baby? Make a free man happy?'

The clue, Kate realized much later, had been there in the expression she glimpsed in Bella's face as Ari left the office. At the time, she interpreted it as resentment that her newly-released husband should make such an open play for a whitey wench. Had she instead read the look as concern over the man himself, Kate just might have gone out looking for him when he didn't return. Had she been quick enough, she just might have seen him trotting away into the night, his sling discarded, his heavy stick no longer used for support but clutched instead like a weapon.

The body was found early next morning on wasteland near a development site by the river. Forensic scientists found evidence of a ferocious struggle: traces of woollen fibres, hair and human skin under the fingernails, knuckles severely split, blood of the assailant's group matted along with the victim's in his clothing.

The pathologist put down the primary cause of death to asphyxiation caused by the heavy ebony walking-stick which had been thrust down the victim's throat; the secondary cause of death he attributed to the stick's having been rammed in with such force that its end had penetrated right down to puncture the liver. Other medical findings included an injury to the back of the neck inflicted by a heavy piece of rusty iron; also acute bruising to the knees, shoulders and arms; also the left eye gouged half out of its socket.

Scene-of-crime investigations also produced a witness, albeit of doubtful value, in the person of an old wino called Spud who had been sleeping rough in discarded drainpipes on the edge of the wasteland. He had heard the fight—bellows of rage and pain mingled with mocking threats and abuse—and had crept close enough to glimpse something of the slaughter. However, at this point Spud's evidence became increasingly fanciful, the man rambling on about the two antagonists seeming to fly and grapple in the air, bounding with almost dance-like leaps into each other, their cries taking on the fiendish quality of some awful chorus of devils. Soon, with the discordant clamour hammering into his head, he had fled in terror of his life—a fairly routine outcome, he had to admit, of his daily hooch consumption.

He was taken to the mortuary by a divisional CID sergeant and shown the victim's corpse on the slender chance it might stir some further memories. It didn't. On the contrary, it merely reduced the old soak to a renewed attack of terror and shakes. Gagging in revulsion, he lurched wildly away to escape the awful sight, only to stumble into the man's widow as she arrived to make the formal identification.

Fortunately for Bella, she had Leena and Winston on either side of her, the two lunging forward to deflect the shocked vagrant away from her. Bella, however, barely noticed, so extreme was her distress, grief and guilt.

CHAPTER 12

Superintendent Barker heard it on the car radio on his way to the Yard: dramatic viceland killing of notorious black pimp, Aristotle Edwards, found brutally murdered barely twelve hours after walking free from Wormwood Scrubs prison . . . released after the appeal court cleared him of the 1985 murder of prostitute Arlene Milton . . . keen speculation in the vice world that he was brutally done to death by the real murderer of Arlene Milton, the killer intent on silencing Edwards before he could seek vengeance for his seven years' wrongful imprisonment . . . speculation also of a link between this murder and the death of Mandy Trotter, another prostitute, whose mutilated remains were unearthed in Berkshire woodland last month . . . however, a different interpretation advanced by the victim's distraught widow, Councillor Bella Edwards, who this morning angrily labelled her husband's death as a vendetta killing by the police. 'They framed Ari in the first place,' she told reporters, 'which is why they've always fought any new investigation and now silenced him. They're trying to bury the truth forever.'

Barker was drenched once again in sweat, his eyes watering, his hands clamped on the wheel. Would the dreadful nightmare never end? Worse, true to all nightmares, he felt utterly powerless to act, unable to check its awful progress. He well knew what response he'd get if he contacted that bastard at Lystons. Worse, if he tried to blow the whistle on them, they would retaliate by implicating him, most probably as an accessory to murder. Worse even than that, they could well send a hit man to silence him once and for all!

Briefly, he considered contacting that Welsh bastard. But no, there could be no compromises with DCI Roberts and therefore no lessening of the risks. The only course was to keep his head down, sit tight and sweat out the living nightmare.

Taff was another who heard the news on his way to work, in fact telephoned on his car-phone by Kate who had heard about it from the ITN news desk. He was surprised less by the black man's death than by how upset Kate sounded over it.

'What's wrong, love? He wasn't the most savoury of characters. Nothing but a parasite—corrupt, catering to men's lust, exploiting women or, more likely, mere girls, taking from life and contributing nothing. Forget him.'

'God's sake, Taff!'

'What's wrong?'

'How can you possibly make such a judgement—especially after he'd sweated out all those years in the nick for a crime of which he wasn't guilty!'

'*May* not have been guilty . . .'

'For Pete's sake, if that's what you think, why go to such lengths to get him out? I mean . . .'

'I don't know what I think—not about Ari Edwards. What matters is the principle of the thing.'

'Oh boy!'

'Listen, Katie, don't let's get into a hassle over this. You met Edwards in very different circumstances from me. Maybe he had a whole lot going for him, I don't know. All I can say, going on the facts as I know them, he was just another pimp.'

'According to Mandy, he was a rather exceptional pimp.' She paused, grimacing in irony. 'The point, don't you see, is that if we'd only *listened* to him right at the start—if Bella and Randi and I had done what he told us about withdrawing Mandy's evidence and leaving the whole issue alone—the poor sod would be alive now! Mandy as well in all probability. But no, we all of us had priorities—the hot story for me, Bella after votes in the election, Randi looking for the big-deal case. Selfish opportunists, all three!'

'It's a dog-eat-dog world, my love.' She didn't reply, and he realized he could have found a more soothing platitude for her conscience. 'Listen, whatever the rights and wrongs of it, I reckon Ari's number was up anyway. Inside prison or out, he was for it.'

The Mandy Trotter murder team had anyway been overdue for a progress review on the case; but now Ari's death gave it priority. They met in the incident room, Chiefie Marsh supervising the reports from Taff and his joint investigating officer, Rob Smith. Despite the coffee and biscuits and Ralph Marsh's pipe-smoke, the atmosphere was far from relaxed, Taff still drawing suspicion.

'You had something to do with getting Edwards released, David, correct?'

'Me, sir?' He managed a rueful grin. 'The day I can manipulate the Court of Appeal, I'll . . .'

'Spare us the wisecracks. Somebody sold it to the DPP. All right, I'm not asking you who it was. But we should know if there's any information we can contribute to the Met's investigation of this latest murder.'

'Er, excuse me, guv'nor, is this from you or are the Met actually asking?'

'I told you, didn't I, Rob,' the super grunted in exasperation to the other officer. 'Dead light on his feet.'

The simple answer on this occasion was that Taff had already compromised his position when he agreed the tacit deal in the swimming-pool with Barker. That the deal had now led to yet another gruesomely mutilated corpse had of course compromised him even more.

'All we can tell them with any degree of certainty, guv'nor, is that the two murders are linked, both probably committed by the same killer. If you want to offer them the Trotter file, fair enough, it's good PR. They might even pick up something from the MO, although the way I heard it, Edwards put up one hell of a fight, so I rather doubt—'

'Heard it from where?' Being of Welsh origins himself, it deeply irritated Ralph Marsh the way Roberts always had to be such a clever-dick. 'Come on, damn it.'

'I had ITN phoning me for details,' Taff conceded. 'As it was, they—er, Kate—knew more than I did. Don't ask me ITN's source, but they seemed to know quite a lot of the forensic findings as well as injury details.'

'Go on.'

'It's thought Edwards may have been lured to a rendez-vous with the killer, possibly to exact vengeance for the murder of Mandy Trotter. However, the forensic people reckon Edwards took a massive whack across the back of the head with a piece of iron. Maybe the killer thought

Edwards was already dead or maybe his idea was to get him somewhere quiet and then finish him off. Whichever, the theory the K Division team are working on is that Edwards must have recovered consciousness and started to fight back—fairly effectively, too, to judge from the forensic findings. He'd left to keep the rendezvous soon after nine-thirty in the evening, and the doc has put time of death at between ten-fifteen and ten-forty-five. So it could have been a fairly drawn-out fight or else Edwards took a long time dying. Since he was skewered almost end to end on his own walking-stick, the latter seems unlikely, despite his being a very tough cookie.'

Both Marsh and Rob Smith were eyeing him askance. Although neither was in any sense unfamiliar with violence and death, both were sickened by this latest outrage.

'A rendezvous?'

'Kate's sure of it.' Then, at their puzzled looks: 'To that extent, Kate's a material witness. She was covering the story at the community centre when Edwards took a call from someone called Perry, Gerry or Terry. Edwards pretended he was going for a leak but never came back. Moreover, from the look she noticed on Bella's face, Kate reckons she *knew* where he was going.'

'Could you swear to that, Miss Lewis?'

'Well, I suppose so, for what it's worth.'

The K Division WDS eyed her in uncertainty. 'How do you mean?'

'Sworn or not, it won't carry much weight as evidence in court.'

'In court? Are you suggesting she's an accessory to her husband's murder?'

Kate groaned in equivocation. 'Obviously, I wouldn't want to put it as strongly as that.'

'How would you put it, then?'

For all her politeness, the woman sergeant was subtly insistent. A pretty effective technique, Kate thought, wondering how it would compare with Taff's interview style under similar circumstances.

'Look, I could well have misread it. Bella might simply have been resentful that he'd just made a pass at me.'

'Had he?'

'No! Just a bit of kidding around.' To her irritation the policewoman jotted down a note of it.

'Yes?'

'Look, Bella Edwards could as easily have been anxious at the extent of his limp or at the amount he'd had to drink. Anything. It certainly didn't have to be conspiracy to murder.'

'It would hardly have been the drink, Miss Lewis. The victim's blood-alcohol reading was minimal.'

'Really?' It was Kate's turn to frown in surprise. Her impression had been strongly to the contrary. 'What about drugs?'

'Totally clear, according to the path report.'

Right, Kate thought, so Ari was expecting that call and had kept his head good and clear in readiness for it, presumably intent on vengeance. Moreover, it seemed likely Bella knew he was expecting it, in which case she might well know who it was from and could identify the mysterious Perry-Gerry-Terry.

The WDS had moved aside to answer an incoming call, only to put the caller on hold and turn in frustration to Kate. 'Any chance you might know where we'd find Councillor Edwards?'

'Bella? Why?'

'When they took her to the hospital mortuary to ID the remains, she went totally to pieces—or appeared to—weeping and yelling all that venomous stuff about how it was a police vendetta killing.' The sergeant sniffed, scratching in irritation at her thick blonde hair. 'Frankly, if it had been down to me, I'd have brought her in for questioning and a statement then and there—if only to keep her away from the press until she'd calmed down. But my DI's hypersensitive about charges of racism. He agreed to let them take her off for a while to recover before questioning. More fool him. I've got him on the line now from the community centre saying there's no sign of her—nor any of her FAME people either.'

'Another deal, Taff old mate?' Jack Walsh shook his head in irony at his one-time partner. 'You do too many deals. You're getting to be more like an old Yard horse-trader than a Welsh crusader.'

'I don't want to be either, Jack, you know that.' He gestured around Walsh's office at the electronic hardware recently returned from the Yard. 'Have you checked all this stuff for bugs?'

'As best I can, yes.' He winked, putting a finger to his lips before gesturing towards the door. 'Fancy a pint?'

'You'd have done the same deal as me with Alec Barker,' Taff remarked once they were clear of the office. 'For a start, I had nothing really solid on him. Also, the force can do without any more corruption scandals like that. There's no way the stupid idiot's going to so much as fiddle his mileage in future, let alone try and stitch characters like Edwards.'

'Such clemency,' Foxy remarked, eyeing him askance. 'Root out the rot at senior level, that used to be your cry. You going through the change or what?'

'The way Barker told it me,' the younger man muttered ruefully, 'he was the victim of an occupational disease known as Vice. Yeah, yeah, I know someone's got to do the dirty work and there's no excuse for yielding to the lusts of the flesh. But that's what he told me, standing there surrounded by swimming kiddies. His was the classic fall: they lured him way off limits, then put the screws on him.' He waved two ironic fingers at the ex-chiefie. 'Of course, you and I would have had more sense, ha-ha. Had *we* been so naïve as to be lured into the tender trap, we'd have reported the blackmailers, then helped trap them in return —in the process saying goodbye to Dell and Kate and whatever else remained of our private lives.'

He nodded, gesturing to pre-empt Walsh's response as they stepped into the lift. 'So I've gone soft. The fact is, I'm still not fully recovered from my three-year stretch on Indecency, so Lord knows how I'd respond to Vice. I just pray to God and the chief constable I'll never have to find out.'

'All right, son, all right.' Foxy nodded, mindful of one or two skeletons in his own closet. 'So at last you're approaching the age of tolerance in your odyssey through the force. About time.' He punched him affectionately on the shoulder. 'Any road, from what you say, you obviously don't see Barker as an accessory to the Edwards killing.'

'No. No doubt he's running witless because of it. But not as an accessory *before* the event.'

'Right.' The retired chiefie grinned in satisfaction, head on one side as they stepped out of the lift at the parking level and started towards his car. 'So a little bit of concerted pressure just might break him . . .' He realized his carphone was ringing and dived to unlock the door and answer it. 'Yes, Kate, yes. Hang on, here he is.'

'Taff, I'm honouring our agreement here.' Taff could tell from Kate's tone that she was excited. 'Bella went walkabout with the FAME team—which, so far as the divisional CID are concerned, makes her and them suspect. I just got a call from her for a meet, but strictly solo.'

'No way. You tell me where or—'

'Listen to Mr Macho! Didn't I say I was keeping our agreement? Now then, meet me outside the north entrance of the Albert Hall soon as you can and we'll work something out.'

Walsh already had them heading for the car park exit, glancing at Taff in curiosity as he turned west. 'Bella Edwards, huh.'

'Sussed of complicity in hubby's death.'

'Right.' Foxy leered at him before braking the big Volvo to a halt. 'Hang on here while I nip back to the office for a wire for Kate to wear.'

Walsh was back within a couple of minutes with the

miniaturized body mike and transmitter, his grin as ironic as ever.

'Of course,' he chuckled, 'it was bloody obvious about Madam Bella. That poor husband of hers was only of use to her while he was in the nick.' He nosed the car into the traffic flow, then added: 'The very last thing she wanted was for you to get the begger out of prison!'

Kate stood in the centre of the Albert Memorial feeling vaguely absurd. The spring sunshine had brought the sight-seers out in droves to stroll among the early daffs and late crocuses. Already she had been snapped twice by Japanese tourists, one of whom had mistaken her for an official who could please inform about implessive marble ediflice.

She could see Jack Walsh's Volvo parked across in front of the Albert Hall. So far she had seen a traffic warden and a policeman tell them to move along, both seemingly satisfied by a wave of Taff's warrant card. She could also communicate one-way via the wire they'd given her. She knew it was working all right at this distance because, when she'd asked him to, Foxy had flashed his lights in answer. She just hoped to goodness Bella hadn't been setting her up when she phoned her for the meet. Nothing would surprise her with that devious lady.

Seeing yet another Jap tourist bearing down on her, Kate wandered off towards a nearby peanut vendor, his stall besieged with pigeons. Bella must have been watching, for she suddenly hurried close to intercept her. As always, she was dressed to be noticed; today's combination of black slacks, black sweater, black beret, dark glasses and violet trainers put Kate in mind of a French TV commercial.

'Where's your cop boyfriend, baby?'

'You said to come alone!'

'Sure, sure, take it easy, OK.' She looked far from easy herself, tense and watchful. 'I figure the Law's after me by now. That right, is it?' Then, when Kate hesitated: 'You heard what I said to those reporters at the mortuary. Vendetta killing, right? No way are the pigs going to take that, least of all from a big-mouth mama like me. They'd have pulled me in when I said it 'cept that inspector pig got scared for his job.' She gave a snort of laughter. 'He'll be even more scared, time we're through.'

'Why?' Kate moved closer so as to be sure the answer reached Taff. 'Just what are you at here?'

'Simple justice, baby.' Bella took a pack of peanuts, scattering them piecemeal for the clamouring pigeons. 'Seven years the man lets my man rot. And what thanks does Ari get? A stick down his gullet! OK, that's his number. Ain't no way FAME's going to sit back and let him walk around a free man—not any more.'

Nor a live man either, Kate thought, to judge from the malevolence in Bella's tone. The black woman was intensely strung up. Yet not with Speed or any other form of drug; this was the same aggressive vigour which had powered her freedom campaign into a major community enterprise and, via local politics, had recently won her nomination as the official candidate in the impending general election.

'This is your sense of guilt talking here, right, Bella?' Then, at the black woman's startled frown: 'If you and me and Randi had all done what Ari told us—if we'd dropped this whole thing at the Mandy stage instead of going for the main chance . . .'

She didn't need to finish. Bella's groan startled the pigeons as she slumped back on to a nearby bench, head lolling forward as the remorse struck. 'Me the worst, huh. Me the soul-damn worst!' She started to rock back and forth, still groaning. 'That Mandy—that kid Mandy . . . let me tell yer, she saw nothing that night . . . *nothing*. She was nowhere near Arlene's place. Just—she just told you all what I schooled her to say!'

'Mandy lied?' For all Kate's suspicions at the time, the girl's murder had seemed totally to confirm her validity as a witness. Now it came as an appalling shock to hear the

whole thing had been no more than an elaborate pretence.
And no wonder—no wonder bloody Bella's sense of guilt!

'So what did you pay her? Thirty pieces of silver?'

'Ha!' A shard of bitterness brought her face up at last.
'Honey, she was so damn cheap, she barely cost a thing!
Guess why, can you? The little tramp had gotten hooked
on something that wouldn't give her no rest—and I don't
mean the junk she was sniffing either. But she didn't know
that that something wasn't mine to give—not any more. So
when I offered it to her for the price of a little perjury, she
just freaked. Yeah, Bella, yeah, yeah, yeah!' She gestured,
pointing at Kate. 'You guessed it, huh?'

'Thinking about it now, yes. In fact, Mandy partly told
me, except I didn't realize it at the time.'

'Right!' She wiped tears angrily from her eyes then jerked
a thumb towards the sunlit sky. 'And now she finally got
the poor bastard. Up there or else down below—whichever
place it is that whores and whoremasters end up in!'

'It—I have to say, it strikes me as odd, given the sort of,
er, business relationship they shared.'

'Like I said to you, with Missie Mandy the man was
crazy soft. As for her? What you need to understand about
kids like her, they're born victims. They're abused so rotten
you wouldn't believe. The day they arrive in this lousy
world it starts and it just gets worse and worse and worse.
So, when some big strong daddy like Ari comes along who's
prepared to value them and talk sweet to them and help
them, why they'll do anything. They'll go into total slavery
for them if that's what's asked. That—OK, that's how
come he owned Mandy. But I tell you something weird, it
wasn't all the one way. It was like he changed as well.
Instead of getting to be a brute like—well, like you'd have
expected of the man, it changed him for the better. It
seemed—would you believe, it seemed to bring out the
goddam father in him. Can you beat that? As near to love
as he could have gotten, if you ask me.'

She took a kick at a cock pigeon as it strutted close in
pursuit of a mate. 'So there, the kid didn't know it, but

she'd got him already. So when old Bella comes telling her, here's a chance to get him out that place and into your arms, honey-child—hell, there was no holding her!'

Kate moved at last to sit beside her on the bench. Ironic, she thought, that the black woman's moment of cathartic intimacy had been shared by the two men in the car, doubtless even now embellishing it with their own cynical observations.

'Bella, why tell me all this? It's hardly for publication, so . . .'

'We need help to find the devil. We got a big long stick with his name on . . .'

'Gerry?'

'Terry. Terry Evil Whittal.'

'How come you know him?'

'I met him once with Ari. He was hustling up clients from some casino. Well, now we gonna de-liver that stick down the devil's throat—down, down, down—till he looks like a little ginger-haired sucking pig on a spit.' She turned to poke abruptly at Kate. 'You're gonna help us, Miss Lewis. You're gonna do it 'cos you got a piece of that guilt along with Randi and me, and this is your chance to avenge my Ari's death. Right?'

'Help how?'

'We put the word out. Half of Brixton's in the search. Everyone who knows anyone in the vice business, in drugs, in protection, even just blaggers and muggers—the whole crime scene—all asking around. Like I'm asking you to do the same with your underworld snouts—every grass on ITN's books, OK—*find Terry Whittal!*'

She broke off in response to a piercing whistle, turning to stare across the park before hopping on to the bench to wave her arms as she returned the whistle. Moments later they saw Winston racing through the trees. Bella whistled again, vaulted down and ran to meet him. Kate, although she wasn't quick enough in pursuit to catch Winston's message, barely needed to; it was obvious from Bella's clenched fists and the gleam in her eyes that they had now got the vital lead.

'Forget it, baby,' she called, waving her away. 'If we don't get lucky, I'll get back to you.' With which she turned and settled into a fast, long-striding jog behind Winston as he headed towards the north side of the park.

'So much for Terry,' Kate remarked to Foxy and Taff on the other end of the wire. It took her a while to reach the memorial and then dodge her way between the traffic along Kensington Gore. When she finally reached the Volvo, it came as little surprise to find Walsh sitting alone behind the wheel.

'Taff'll have to be fit to keep those two in sight,' she remarked, hopping in as Foxy gunned the engine and swung them sharply into the westerly traffic flow.

'In any event, things could get very sticky for this Terry geezer,' Walsh chuckled, sliding her a sardonic wink. 'He could face a sticky end—literally.'

The trail, in the form of the FAME minibus, led them to a partly-built industrial estate on a site between the M4 and Hayes. They had picked Taff up on the Hyde Park ring road near Victoria Gate and then, thanks to some creative driving by Walsh, caught up with the brightly-striped minibus at the far end of Notting Hill.

From concealment near the entrance to the estate, they watched the FAME team search cautiously across towards the one fully completed building on the further side of the estate. From its structure, it appeared to be a windowless hangar of a place, destined perhaps to become a wholesaling outlet, but as yet little more than a cavernous shell. Around it were similar constructions, mostly at the bare-girder stage, rising like dinosaur frames from a sea of puddled clay.

'You're on the run and hiding out in a half-built industrial estate when a bunch of vengeful Afro-Caribbeans come to get you. Discuss at least three possible options.'

'Hang on.' Walsh grinned. 'Let's take it a stage earlier

than that. You're on the run from a bunch of vengeful Afro-Caribbeans; what steps do you take to survive?'

'I simply do not believe this!' Kate cut in. 'Playing silly games when at the very least you should be calling for back-up!'

'You're operating off limits,' Taff murmured in reply, 'unauthorized and in company with a member of the popular press. You're following a distinctly thin lead based on tenuous assumptions and involving six law-abiding ethnic-minority citizens who are seen to enter a deserted building site. Discuss . . .'

'Option one,' Kate snapped, 'think about saving some lives!'

Taff shrugged, leaning across to hand her the mobile phone. 'Call up ITN for a camera crew by all means. They're bound to get some good visuals of the FAME team whether or not Terry's in there.'

Walsh waited until Kate was busy with the phone, then pointed out that, despite all the heavy plant and materials littering the site, the gates were unlocked and open, the site office dark and the place devoid of security personnel. 'It's all just a shade too convenient, huh.'

'Right.' Taff was already easing out of the vehicle. 'Stay with the lady.'

Not entirely to his surprise, he found the door of the Portakabin office unlocked and, searching around, eventually found the site guard locked in a cupboard and strapped around with wrapping tape like a plastic latter-day mummy. Due to his severely restricted breathing, the man was puce-faced and comatose, so that Taff had to spend desperate minutes unwrapping and then breathing fresh life back into him. Predictably, when he at last dashed to the phone, he found the wires cut.

He raced from the office to use Walsh's car-phone. Midway, however, he was checked by the distant whoomph of errupting gasoline. Swinging round, he saw a figure dash from the hangar entrance, then slam and secure the big doors. The same moment, a white van revved to life at the further side of the site and swung fast towards the hangar.

In view of the distance, Taff decided to bellow out *Terry!* as loudly as he could then ran forward. The man checked in alarm before turning to race towards the van. But for his panic at Taff's shout, he might have realized in time to dodge aside; as it was, far from slowing as expected, the van accelerated. Still heading wildly forward, the man tried too late to lunge aside, slipped in the mud and went down under the wheels of the speeding vehicle.

Instantly, the van slithered to a halt, then reversed back over the body before slamming into forward gear to drive over it yet again. Then, seeing Taff, the van driver switched on his headlights and slammed a hand on the horn, leaving the copper in no doubt he'd be run down as well unless he cleared out of the way. Taff tried for a look at the driver's face, but he raised a hand as he roared past. Next second, slewing wildly to one side, he whacked into the Volvo's offside wing as Walsh tried to head him off. However, wheels slithering in the mud, the van managed to skid clear and head for the site exit. Walsh tried to turn and give chase, but bogged down in the rutted clay alongside the main access track.

Meanwhile, glancing back at the hangar, Taff saw the sinister plumes of black smock billowing from the eaves. He sprinted across to drag the heavy bolts aside and heave the doors open. Flames billowed fiercely out at the top, promptly followed by the first of the FAME team, hunched low and choking wildly from the fumes. Taff counted them out one after the other, each one reeling and gasping. He was about to crawl in in search of the last two when the figure of Winston fell out backwards, his clothing singed and smouldering, his hands locked around those of the unconscious Bella.

Taff ran to drag her clear. As he knelt to give her the kiss of life, he noticed the gaping flesh wound at the back of her head. Next moment, black hands tugged him aside and Leena crawled close to put her mouth to Bella's.

Taff fell back in relief, heaving to retrieve his own breath

—only to register the presence of the ITN camera team in action behind them. Ruefully, he reflected that this was one media stunt even Bella couldn't have bettered.

CHAPTER 13

DCI Andy Clough of K Division arrived in a high-profile cavalcade of ambulances and police cars, lights flashing and sirens blaring. Taff half-expected dark-glasses and a Beverly Hills drawl, but the man turned out to be a laid-back South Londoner.

'We just found the white van abandoned in Southall,' he remarked to Taff. 'If you'd called us a bit earlier we might have collared the driver.'

'It's, er, never an easy decision.'

'Us being the Met, you mean? You whistle up ITN but not us.' He grimaced. 'I'd heard about you before but I always thought it must be malicious gossip.'

Taff gestured apology, for once at a loss. But curiously enough the DCI seemed more amused than reproachful. 'So what'll you give me to keep it quiet? What's on offer?'

'How about some useful stuff on the Ari Edwards murder?'

Clough pointed at him, conceding a nod. 'That was the one good thing I heard about you: always ready to trade.'

'Something I learned with the Met,' Taff quipped, leading him across to where the forensic experts and photographer were getting busy around the corpse of the small ginger-haired man crushed into the mud.

'Meet Terry Whittal. According to Bella, he's the torture artist who did for Arlene Milton and little Mandy Trotter. My bet is, the path lab will find there's a tissue match with the skin fragments they found under Ari Edwards's finger nails this morning—also the post-mortem should reveal injuries sustained during their fight last night.'

'Just one question, you clever bastard,' the Met officer asked, head on one side, 'who gets the credit?'

'It's your patch, your team and your conclusions.' Taff winked, jerking a thumb towards the ITN crew. 'Why don't you just step over to the camera and claim the glory right now? Thames Valley will be happy to settle for the Trotter murder.'

'It's a deal.' He nodded again, then gave Taff a sidelong glance. 'One thing: what do we do about the Arlene Milton case?' Then, when Taff frowned in uncertainty: 'I've already had a rather tense Chiefie Barker ringing me from the Yard and asking chapter and verse on the Edwards murder.'

'Tell you what.' Taff grinned, wishing all Met officers could be as frank as this one. 'Collaborate with me on the Milton case and I'll help you find the hit-and-run merchant in the white van.'

At which point, finding this whole business of trading murder collars and clear-ups absurdly over the top, both chief inspectors started to snort with laughter—a reaction which, to their mutual chagrin, the ITN camera-man managed to catch on a zoom lens and later transmit to millions of fascinated viewers.

Kate was barely into the news room before the researcher pounced. 'Miss Lewis—'

'We have a major story on the go, Harley. Whatever it is had better be good.'

'In two words: Janine McKane.'

Kate spun in her tracks and came back to him. 'You got me.'

'She rang ten minutes ago. I told her you were on your way in from Hayes with an exclusive, but she said she'd be in the Leicester Square McDonalds for half an hour and no more. She said if you can make it—totally on your own— that's fine. Otherwise, forget it.'

'Oh boy.' She was already leading him away from the news room. 'Don't say a word about this to Mr Cawley.'

'I already did.' Then, with exaggerated casualness: 'He said not to tell you but to leave that to him.'

'Right on,' Kate chuckled, warming increasingly to the media graduate. 'So if he asks, say I beat it out of you and I've taken ex-Chiefie Walsh along as chaperon.'

'She won't show if he's—'

'Idiot, she won't see him.'

The inspector at the Yard's central bureau stared stubbornly at the two chief inspectors and shook his head. 'You two should know the regulations regarding the informants' fund. Absolutely no access without the authority of the original investigating officer. In this instance, that's Chief Superintendent Barker.' He reached doubtfully for a telephone. 'If you like, I can try and contact him . . .'

'Don't bother.' Andy Clough handed him a document. 'Here's your authority.'

'A flaming warrant?' The inspector stared at it, amazed. 'What the bloody hell . . . ?'

'Fully in order,' Taff remarked. 'Signed by the Marylebone stipendiary magistrate, specifying date and circumstances. That unquestionably over-rides Mr Barker's authority.' He gestured towards the filing room. 'Hurry it up, Inspector.'

The man studied the warrant for a moment or two, shaking his head over it in open disapproval yet bound to accept its force. He reached for the phone again, then changed his mind and headed gloomily for the files. Although flushed when he went, he was scarlet when he returned a few minutes later. He carried a large register open at mid-August 1985. Visibly shocked, he laid it before them and shook his head.

'Gone. Twentieth of August, missing. Whole page.' He pointed to where the torn edges of the adjoining page were visible along the spine. 'Gone, for Pete's sake!'

'You keep a record of everyone who refers to this fund file?'

'We keep a note of all the authorizations, yes, of course.'

'Then I suggest you start looking through for any signed by either Alec Barker or else Commander Hammond. Send a written report of your findings to DCI Clough at K Division. Include a note of your views on how that page could possibly have been removed without your knowledge.' The man went to reply, but Taff stopped him. 'Not now, Inspector. Just state it all in the report, plus a copy to me at Thames Valley HQ.'

Kate knew who to look for, having brought her copy of the photograph produced as Crown evidence at Ari's trial: Janine and Arlene together as snapped by the camera concealed in Arlene's place. As yet, however, she could see no sign of anyone remotely resembling Janine McKane.

She bought a milkshake, then moved to sit as near as she could to the window, hoping that would boost reception for Jack Walsh via the wire she was again wearing.

She sipped her drink for a while, pretending to read a newspaper but in fact trying to control her breathing and calm down. It was absurd to let it get her so wound up; there was no possible danger, least of all with Walsh listening to it all in his car just around the corner. Yet the shock of that last awful rendezvous in dockland was still too recent.

'S'cuse me.'

Kate jumped, then shook her head at the woman standing beside the table with a tray. 'Sorry, I'm expecting someone to join me.'

The woman nodded. 'That'd be Janine, right, Miss Lewis?'

Kate looked more closely. It wasn't only the hairstyle and colouring that were totally different, the whole face seemed more pointed and there was even a different tilt to the nose. And yet, yes, now that she really looked for it, the likeness was there.

'Either you're Janine's sister or you've changed a great deal in seven years.'

'I've bloody aged, for sure.' She had a strong Scots accent and, despite her short, black-dyed hair, Kate could see the freckled skin to match the copious auburn hair of the photograph. She sat down with her back to the window and lit a cigarette to go with the coffee she'd brought across. 'Promise you're no' trying to snatch any pics, eh?'

'No. But I don't see what you've got to be so nervous about.'

'Ah!' The scorn broke from her like a cry for help. 'Get you, Miss Fancy Lewis. You have *them* after you and see how nervous y'are.'

'All right.' She gestured in dismissal. 'But where's the point in a secret meeting like this?'

'Och, there's a point tae it, though much good it'll do anyone.' She guffawed, shaking her head. 'Call it seven years of conscience. Seven years of needing to bloody share it, that's the point.'

'First Mandy Trotter's death and now Ari's—is that what's pricked up your conscience?' Then, when Janine merely scowled at her: 'If it's anything to you, Terry Whittal's dead as well. He was killed this afternoon.'

'Huh?' Clearly, from the blankness of Janine's expression, it wasn't anything to her. 'How should that be good?'

'Whittal was an unscrupulous East London crook-cum-psychopath. Almost certainly, he was the one who tortured Arlene to death, also Mandy, and then last night killed Ari Edwards.' She gave a wry snort. 'He also at one time set me up to get raped and then tried his damnedest to run me down in his Range-Rover. Not someone I intend to grieve for.'

Janine nodded sombrely. 'Sounds like the stroppy ned I once had a conversation with. Luckily for me, it was over the phone or I'd likely be dead as the rest of them.' She paused to draw tensely on her cigarette. 'See, most of that stuff they said about me during the trial was right enough. What they didn't say was that it was nae poor Arlene Milton but me who set it up. You could say it all began with the pair of us working as hostesses in Blandells Casino. Then Arlene got taken up by big Ari and in no time she

became one of his main girls. But I'd still see her 'cos he
kept her working the Blandells patch. That's how I noticed
the customers he was pulling for her were mostly very
upmarket. Ye ken what I mean: very well-heeled, often
faces in the news, people like that.'

She paused to light another fag from the stub of the other,
puffing at it before resuming with a curt shake of her head.
'If I could just have been born simple 'stead of canny, eh.
But there it is: if, if, if. Any road, the crunch came when I
got the push from Blandells. They accused me of thieving,
but the *real* reason was 'cos I refused to screw with their
bloody punters. And, boy, did I resent that! It was then I
told her: Arlene kiddie, I said, you're missing out on a
gold-mine with some of them big nobs you're entertaining.
If we could just work it so's to snap a few action pics of
them, we could land ourselves some very handy dosh.'

'Blackmail, you mean?'

'To tell you the truth, I told her we'd be safer selling to
the Sunday papers or else *Private Eye* or the like. But the
hell of it is, we never even got that far. Someone was ahead
of us with the idea. OK, maybe it was her pimp Ari. Maybe
it was this guy Terry Whittal. But I've thought and thought
about it ever since and my guess is it was more likely Lystons, being as they were nearly all Blandells customers she
was pulling.'

Janine paused, grimacing in irony as Kate handed her
the copy of the trial photograph. 'Christ, the shock when I
first saw that in the papers! Mind you, I'd already had the
phone call long before that. It must have been the day after
her death—this guy on the line, trying to fix a date. Luckily,
being a canny lass, I didna go for it, just kept asking who
he was. Then he lost his rag and said Arlene had give him
my number and I'd best get away out of sight because, see
here, if I didn't, I'd have the Mob tae reckon with. Aye,
that's what he said: the Mob.'

'As in Mafia?'

'Aye, well that's what made me think it must be Lystons
who'd planted that camera. That surprise you does it, Miss

Lewis? Listen, just 'cos they're a flashy public company
that don't mean they're Mob-proof. Merged with that big
hotel and entertainments firm in the States about ten years
ago, ye ken? Well, maybe you wouldn't, but you would if
you'd been working at Blandells at the time. Changed them,
it did. Slow but sure, more and more Yanks in as managers,
pressuring table staff like me to lay the customers, all the
tell-tale signs of money-laundering and that. And no doubt
using other Mob tricks when it suits them. Like hidden
cameras. Like murderous bloody hit men. *Bastards!*'

She shook her head and spread her hands in a wry gesture. 'Now ye ken why I'm not for spouting any of this on
camera. The day I risk a stunt like that, I'm for a slab in
the morgue. Curtains. Same as it was curtains for old Ari
the moment he came out the nick. You lot should have left
him be. He'd be alive now if you'd just left him in there to
carry the can like he has these past six or seven years.'

And *touché* to you, Kate Lewis, the reporter thought ruefully, eyeing Janine with a touch more sympathy. Seven
years with the Mafia threat hanging over her, no wonder
she was thinner in the face. Likely, if she hadn't dyed it,
her hair would have been white by now! 'You're sure it
wasn't Ari Edwards who phoned you with those threats?'

'Certain. I knew Big Ari and I'd have known that boom-
ing voice of his for sure.'

'So, assuming it was Terry Whittal who phoned you, how
come he got hold of your number?'

'It—' she lowered her face, stubbing out the half-smoked
fag—'it had to be Arlene told him. You see, canny again,
eh—I'd taken the precaution of just giving her a number
to call. Nothing else, certainly no address.' She sniffed and
gave a nervous shrug. 'Like I said, if he'd known where tae
find me, that would likely have been me for the body-bag.'

'Later, when they found Arlene's corpse and the whole
murder investigation got under way, didn't you think of at
least phoning in your information to the police?'

'Och aye, sure I thought of it. See, by then I was hiding
out like a wee yellow rat in Clydeside. But no ways. Nor

when the fuzz published yon damned picture and called on
me tae come forward. See, that's when I had the face job
done.' She snorted, gesturing at the slant of her nose. 'I
never much cared for how it was before.'

'And anyway,' Kate exclaimed in exasperation as she got
back into Walsh's Volvo soon after, 'nothing Janine said
really changes anything.'

'It goes a fair way to confirming the motive evidence put
up by the prosecution,' Foxy pointed out. 'No wonder they
tried to get her to come forward and testify.' He nodded,
anticipating Kate's protest. 'OK, I know she said it wasn't
Edwards who threatened her. But since he already knew
her, it follows he'd get someone else to telephone so that
she wouldn't recognize him.'

'Jack, you're not *still* trying to lay it on Ari!'

He chuckled at her, shaking his head. 'Good coppers try
to avoid making judgements; it's their job to assemble and
evaluate all possible evidence.' He nodded. 'And that's one
possible evaluation.'

'OK then, here's another: Janine McKane's a plant.
She was a fiction dreamed up by Barker to provide the
prosecution with a motive at the trial, and now he's sent
us a look-alike to the photo to make—well, to make us
think . . .'

She trailed off, acknowledging the improbability of it.
But no worse than all the other versions worked into the
web of lies and deceits and counter-lies from all and sundry
—from Bella and Alfie Small, from Barker and Ari. All of
them, it seemed, going in terror of the multi-national Lystons with their sinister Mob backing.

'For what it's worth,' Jack murmured, holding up his
camera, 'I managed to snap Janine as she left the big Mac.'

'Brilliant,' Kate nodded, impressed. 'I just wish I could
see some hope of running the real story and nailing
Lystons!'

Judge Willis eyed Taff dourly as he was shown into his office, offering neither handshake nor chair.

'I don't mind telling you, Roberts, but for the phone call on your behalf from Judge Hartington, who I know thinks well of you, I should not have agreed to see you.'

He sniffed, drumming his fingers on the desk. Taff stayed silent, deciding it was best to let Willis unload his reproaches first.

'I have to tell you, all your tampering with the Edwards conviction—worse, siding with that opportunist wife of his, not to mention the despicable television people . . . I honestly don't know what your chief constable's at, letting you carry on like that, I really don't. You certainly did me no favours with all your prying and crusading. It never looks good for a trial judge to have a conviction overturned. Never. No matter about PACE and all the Appeal Court judgements changing the rules, it still reflects poorly. Oh, I know, I know, I'm in good company, what with the Birmingham Six, the Maguires and all the rest of them. But look how it's turnd out! All your blessed crusading, and now the wretched fellow's dead. Well, there it is, I just hope you're satisfied, that's all.' He grunted, shaking his head. 'But obviously you're not or you wouldn't be here now taking up my precious time.'

'Quite right, your honour.'

'So come on, what is it you want?'

'I'm after the people behind it all, sir.'

'The one who ran down this man Whittal?'

'And those behind him, sir. You see, there was reference made during the trial to a police informant. We're trying to identify who it was.'

'So ask Commander Hammond. Ask Superintendent Barker.' Then, seeing Taff's stony look, he groaned in exasperation. 'Oh dear, dear, are there no honest policemen any more?'

'I found a reference in the trial transcript, sir, to your being shown written evidence of the informant's identity.' Taff pulled the transcript from his briefcase and opened it at a marker. 'Produced on the third day of the trial, during Mr Barker's evidence in chief. We tried to check in the informants' fund register—where payments are recorded —but the relevant page had been torn out.'

'You don't say.' The judge promptly heaved to his feet and crossed his office to a panelled cupboard which turned out to be filled with large notebooks. 'So you're hoping I noted down this snout's name, eh?'

'Correct, sir.'

'Are you a betting man, Roberts?'

'Only on certainties, sir.'

'What date did the trial commence?'

Taff told him, impressed to see the speed with which Willis located the relevant volume and leafed through to the third day as he returned to his desk to put on his spectacles and scan through the neat entries. 'I make it my business, you see, to be punctilious in my stewardship of all trials, so I would happily lay odds on . . . Ah, here we are.' He placed a finger on the entry and swivelled it for Taff to read. 'Alan Turnbull. Although I've written down this Islington address, I've put L.H. after it for lodging house, so I suspect that means you've got no more than his name. Can that be of sufficient help to you?'

'It might be, assuming he's an employee of the company we suspect of being behind the whole thing.'

'Ah.' The judge closed the notebook, eyeing the policeman with curiosity. 'That would presumably be Lystons, owners of Blandells Casino from which most of Arlene Milton's clients came.'

Taff nodded, impressed that he should have sussed them. 'We could use you in the CID, sir.'

'Well, of course most trial judges are sleuths at heart. One sits there day after day, hearing evidence of every shade and stripe. A snippet here, a clue there; piece them all together, seek out the pattern.' He gave a little nod of satisfaction. 'Also, don't forget in the Edwards trial I had to rule on whether or not to let him subpœna all these so-called Names.' He grimaced in irony. 'The Cabinet

Bimbo aspect, as the *Eye* labelled it. So the Milton girl's clients, actual and alleged, also the probable source of those clients, namely Blandells Casino, were a matter of prime concern to me in deciding that ruling.'

He shut the notebook and put it away. It was on the tip of Taff's tongue to ask the judge how he had decided his ruling, but there was no need. The recollection alone was enough.

'Oh, I knew very well it was just a shabby defence ploy. Furthermore, they knew I would most probably rule against their request to order those people into the witness-box. Whatever was there to gain, after all? Even if they had been photographed in *flagrante delicto* and then blackmailed, they were hardly going to admit as much in court! But either way, the defence stood to gain. If I refused, then of course they'd wring their hands and shriek injustice; if I allowed it, they'd have paraded a handful of prominent individuals —MPs, bankers, even judges!—through the witness-box. Obvious denials all round, as I say, but a possibility of confusing the issue for the more anti-Establishment jury members.'

He shrugged in irony before resuming. 'The defence submitted their list of prominent names they wanted to call as witnesses; the police checked the names with the Blandells management to see if any were frequenters of the casino.' He shook his head. 'They were not.'

Taff nodded, aware that, frequenters or not, Lystons would have told Chiefie Barker to deny it; after all, having framed Ari Edwards with Arlene's murder, they'd want to be sure the jury found him guilty.

In any event, Taff at last had the link between Barker and Lystons, namely Alan Turnbull—assuming, of course, that Barker had supplied the correct name and not a fictitious one for the punctilious Judge Willis to note in his book. But would they find Alan Turnbull on Lystons' staff list?

Bella was either concussed or drunk. Indeed, the more

they talked, tears and remorse flowing unchecked, the more Kate decided it must be drink. After all, with one of the FAME team constantly on guard near her hospital bedside, it was no problem to get liquor or even drugs to her.

'Something I want you to know,' she whispered after first motioning the guard out of the little ward. 'You know why they tried to kill me?' Then, when Kate hesitated, wondering if Foxy Walsh was picking this up in the hospital car park: 'Same reason they had to kill Ari just as soon as he came out of prison—to silence him.'

'Because of what you know? About Lystons?'

'Lord help us, kid,' she sniffed, clutching Kate's hand, 'if you know that much already, how come they ain't after you and all, huh?'

'They tend to use more sophisticated ways of muzzling the press,' Kate answered bitterly. 'So just what is it you know, Bella?'

'Only what Ari told me,' she muttered through a tissue as she dabbed at her eyes. 'Lay off with all this Free Ari stuff, he told me after the trial. You know why he told me that, Miss Lewis? 'Cos the plain simple fact of it was, the man was guilty!'

'*What?*' After all the hassle, all the campaigning and the final triumph, it seemed a downright obscenity. 'He killed Arlene Milton?'

'No, God's sake, no! Ari wasn't no savage torturing devil! No way, no way! But it's a fact he was round there when Terry Whittal was at her—when the evil pig was questioning her about the photograph, accusing her of trying to get clever with Lystons' customers and all that. Then after Terry sent him to pour some Scotch, he came back to find the bastard done killed her. OK, after that, he—well, he was forced to help get rid of her. Accessory, right. According to the law, that makes him guilty of murder, sure as if he actually struck her dead himself.'

Kate stared in amazement, but less at Ari's role in it— that fitted like a key with what Janine had told her—so much as at Bella's actions. To have wilfully ignored her husband's urgings not to campaign, doing so indeed out of total self-interest and with a cold disregard for her husband's safety, seemed appallingly perverse—especially since he must have told her the Mob were behind Lystons and hence the consequence of defying them.

'No, Miss Lewis,' the woman sobbed, waving her hands at her, 'you've no call to look so accusing. Bella's her own judge here. You're right what you're thinking. Right, right, right!' She groaned, then blew her nose before pointing at her. 'But, see here, there's one thing y'ought to understand: FAME ain't *just* Bella, any more than it was *just* Ari's freedom. FAME was a focus for a whole lot of people, Katie baby; and it was a purpose for a whole mass of folk who see their lives as pretty much hopeless.'

She had ceased crying now. Instead, drunk or sober, she was edging back on to her soap-box. 'FAME gave work to scores of unemployed, and it gave a welfare centre to a whole community. Whatever it done for me, it also gave the black people of Brixton a councillor they can call their very own. You go into public service, baby, you'll begin to know what I'm saying here. Yes, it's true I done wrong. OK, some might say the death of my husband should be laid at my door. But whatever Bella's guilt in it, FAME must go on. Unless—' she paused to raise her clenched fists with a touch of the old aggression—'unless it goes on, don't you see, Miss Lewis—unless it goes on, why then that great laughing hunk of a man just died for nothing.'

Kate went to answer, but Bella grabbed her hands in urgent pleading. 'It's down to you, don't you see, down to you! My man's done and gone for good. But his death already set him up there on that hero's pedestal to live on in the hearts of the oppressed, mourned and cherished as a victim of the whitey Establishment!'

She snorted and dabbed at her eyes, moved by her own oratory. 'Anyway, kid, you know what I'm saying here. If you show him up for what he was—accessory to murder, cowed half out of his life by fear of the Mob—if you show them that side of the man, you can see what you'll do for

FAME. You can see what you'll do for the fine force for good and purpose and unity which it is today, Amen.'

'I asked her about the coppers' nark aspect,' Kate told Taff later, 'and why she'd told Mandy to mention that in her statement. Bella said it was merely what Ari had told her. Apparently Terry Whittal knew Janine had a grievance against Lystons and he suspected her and Arlene of trying to get the dirt on the company—even to the extent of betraying them to the police. Apparently, Whittal got totally obsessed with the idea, getting more and more violent with her until he literally shook her to death.'

Taff grunted, frowning in thought, but Kate persisted. 'Bella also said Whittal was dead scared of fouling things up with Lystons. Apparently, he was like a middle man, hired by Lystons to find reliable fun bunnies for their more special clients. Whittal had done a deal with Ari to produce top-drawer fun bunnies. Later, when the Lystons camera caught Arlene and Janine attempting to set up their own photographic venture, that put a *lot* of egg on Whittal's face. However, when he went too far and killed Arlene, Lystons would have realized there was a risk of the death being linked back to them—big, brass-bound British company rated among the top hundred on the Stock Exchange listing. So the decision was made to throw Ari to the wolves rather than Whittal. Ari came to terms with it, doubtless left in no doubt of the alternative if he refused. Bella, however, launched implacably into FAME—with disastrous consequences.'

'And with due support,' Taff remarked ruefully, 'from the rest of us.'

'Right!'

'Wonderful, eh. All that crusading and arm-twisting, all those threats and deals to get Ari's conviction quashed, and he was *de facto* guilty all the bloody time! Another PACE victory for English justice.'

CHAPTER 14

'Lawrence, that's the *true* story, the facts!'

'And you should know better than to shout that at an editor. We can only publish what we can get away with.' Cawley gave Kate a world-weary grimace then bowed acknowledgement. 'You landed a great piece last night out at that industrial estate, so be content with that. Forget all this libellous stuff about Lystons and the Mafia.'

'But Janine McKane—'

'Said effectively nothing. Try to use this tape-recording and Walsh's photograph as verification, and Lystons' lawyers will take us to the cleaners.' He shook his head. 'Leave it at what we said on *News at Ten* last night: that Whittal tried to do away with the entire FAME squad, only to be murdered by his accomplice in the van. End of terrific story. We'll round it off with a hospital piece from Bella about FAME's future as the Sword of Brixton and that's it, finished.'

'Meanwhile, the evil of organized crime goes unchecked. One of the UK's flagship companies fronting for the Mafia!'

'Kate darling, if you want to be a real crusading journalist—which I know you don't because you're too hooked on being on camera—go and join the *Guardian* or the *Sunday Times*. Anyway, you wouldn't find their lawyers any less nervous of Lystons than ours.'

'Bastard.' Kate's chin was out, deeply resenting the dig that she was hooked on the cameras. 'I could almost believe you've been got at already, Lawrence darling. Or maybe you're just scared of having acid poured over that precious Bentley of yours!'

'Lystons remain unmentioned,' the editor retorted coldly, 'and Ari Edwards remains on course to become rap's best-loved black folk-hero.'

Lystons' head office rose high and opulent above the City streets, an elegant, modern design with a purity of line which belied the dark side of the company's revenues, a gleaming bastion of City probity as refined as its Mafia overlords could wish to see. The majority of those around the boardroom table were still plummy Oxbridge, one of them an ex-Cabinet minister, another a retired chairman of the Betting and Levy Board; however, the boardroom voices with the most force had a decidedly American drawl. Unlike many of its rival companies in the City, the ongoing problem in Lystons' audit department was how best to disperse its profits; in particular, how to absorb the dispro- portionate income from its gambling branch.

Alan Turnbull's office was tucked away on the fifth floor and carried the euphemistic label of Deputy-Assistant Security. Whatever activities this involved, the décor and office equipment gave few clues—no charts or schedules on the walls, nothing more hi-tech than a TV video in one corner. The man himself was clad in an expensive checked suit, a silk shirt and Italian shoes. His boozer's complexion and small piggy eyes were creased with a welcoming grin as he ushered the two men into his office. However, he lost both the grin and all trace of colour when his two visitors produced their warrant cards.

'Mr Turnbull, we're here in connection with the death of Terence James Whittal on a building site in Hayes yes- terday evening.' DCI Clough paused to pull out a note- book before rattling off the caution.

'You're wrong,' Turnbull muttered, staring in shock. 'Wrong.'

'We have grounds to believe you were present at the site,' Taff said.

'Furthermore,' Clough cut in, 'that you drove a white Ford van licence number E779 DGM which you repeatedly drove over Whittal, fatally injuring him before driving off at speed in such a manner as to threaten Chief Inspector Roberts when he attempted to stop you.'

'I want a lawyer.'

'As is your right, sir.' Taff nodded. 'Obviously Lystons have a legal department here in the building.' He moved to lift the telephone, but Turnbull hurriedly checked him.

'No, not them. My own.'

'It's your choice, of course.' Taff slid the telephone across. 'Call him now, go on.'

Turnbull began searching vaguely for a number, then asked in a hoarse voice if they were arresting him.

'That's largely down to you, Mr Turnbull.'

'How?' He managed a lop-sided smirk. 'I don't understand.'

'Assuming you cooperate to the full, sir, there's a possibility we'd find no grounds for an arrest.'

For two officers who had never teamed up before, Clough and Taff were managing a fair double act, the one gruff, the other sympathetic. Had Turnbull not been their sole prospect of cracking into Lystons, Taff could well have enjoyed the cat-and-mouse play.

'Hang about —' Turnbull shook his head—'just what do you mean by cooperate?'

Taff shifted a chair across towards the desk but remained standing. 'You sure you're content to proceed with this here in your office?'

'If he's insisting on a lawyer,' Clough remarked, putting the notebook away, 'we'd be best to make it the station . . .'

'What grounds?' Turnbull cut in, his face no longer pale but flushed with anxiety.

'Sir?'

'*Grounds to believe*, that's what you just said. What grounds?'

'Photographic evidence,' Clough retorted.

'Of what? Let me see it.'

'All in good time, Mr Turnbull. Additionally, there's information from a Scotland Yard officer with whom you have had transactions in the past.'

The man shrugged, repeating the smirk. 'Been several of those.'

'Really, sir?' Clough hauled out the notebook again. 'Namely?'

'Look, what is this? Stop playing games, will you!'

'Hardly games. The murder of Terence Whittal is an extremely grave matter.'

'Extremely,' Taff agreed. 'As are certain other matters in which we believe you may be implicated.'

'Such as?' The process was visibly getting to him, sweat beading his forehead, his hands clamped to keep from twitching. 'What the hell you getting at, eh?'

'Accessory to the murder of Aristotle Edwards the night before last, for one.'

'For another, conspiring to murder Amanda Jane Trotter on or about the tenth of February last.'

'You—you've got to be . . .' Turnbull's voice died in a hoarse gulp.

'Also making threatening telephone calls to a senior police officer.'

'And uttering threats,' Taff added, 'purportedly on behalf of certain senior members of this company.'

'No!' Had he known the interrogation procedures specified in PACE, he'd have realized the two officers were already in breach, using tactics of implicit threats and flagrant harassment. Likewise, he might have guessed they had nothing really solid on him and were hence having to resort to bluff. Fortunately, he was floundering too deeply in panic to realize any such thing. 'Stop giving me the treatment! You're just here to stitch me!'

'No need to stitch, mate,' Clough snapped. 'We've got you bang to rights.'

Taff nodded, but then added quietly, 'Mind you, that's not to say we wouldn't be open to a deal.'

'Deal?' He was shaking his head, his expression that of a man who from supposed perfect health is suddenly given a prognosis of imminent death. 'No chance.'

'Certainly no chance for you, mate—not unless you can come up with the goods. Lystons are the only card you've got left to play.'

'You don't know what you're asking!'

'We know very well,' Taff assured him, his voice lowered in conspiracy. 'If we didn't know what Lystons are up to, we wouldn't even consider a deal. Of course it's not just Lystons we're after but the Mob behind them.'

That did it, at last galvanizing a reaction—although not the cooperation either officer had been hoping for. Instead, they found themselves suddenly staring into the barrel of a heavy calibre automatic pistol. 'Over against the wall!'

'Don't be a prat! Putting yourself outside the law won't help—'

'Over there, I said!'

'Listen, Alan—'

'Move! MOVE!'

But Taff still hesitated, his Welsh stubbornness in conflict with his sense of prudence. The man was not bluffing, of that there seemed little doubt. Indeed, so far as Clough was concerned, there was emphatically no contest, his hands hastily spread against the wall above his head in dread of the bullet. Likewise, Taff knew that his future, his health, his love for Kate—all these were ranged against his obstinate defiance of brute force and lawlessness. Yet to a degree, the former were all part of the latter; for if he relinquished his principles and bottled out, what sort of a future would that leave him? Nor was it a case of reckless heroism. On the contrary, having endured his baptism of violence and pain as a beat bobby in Cardiff's Tiger Bay, Taff Roberts knew a lot more about fear than most people.

'Think it out,' he persisted evenly. 'It's not *you* we want, it's bloody Lystons. If you go on the run from us now, you'll have the Mob after you as well. Obviously you will. There's no way they can leave you at large. They'll have a contract out on you just as surely as you had to rub out Terry Whittal. The Mob trade in greed and fear, not loyalty. You're just dog's meat to them.'

It was impossible to tell whether his words were getting through. The man's expression was frozen with shock, the erratic trembling of the gun barrel the sole reaction indicator. Yet there was no challenging the force of Taff's logic.

'Put yourself outside the law and you're as dead as Ari Edwards and Terry. Turn supergrass on them, and you'll have police protection, the guarantee of a new identity and the prospect of a new life at the end of it all.'

Turnball again waved the gun, gesturing for him to turn to the wall, but Taff continued to stare him out. 'Don't be a burk! Give yourself a chance. Put the gun on the desk and the three of us'll walk out of here as casually as if we're going down the boozer for a session.' Pause, Turnbull still shaking with shock. 'It's your only chance. You know that.'

'Supergrass, for Pete's sake . . .'

'The system's well geared up to it now,' Taff assured him. 'They've got a special high-security unit at Reading Prison. Underground it is and done up like a blessed country club.'

'Underground or not,' Turnbull whispered, 'the Mob can get you *anywhere*. No hiding-place!'

'I hear what you say, Alan, but I repeat, it's your only chance.'

There was a long pause, the man and his gun still trembling. 'Right then,' he muttered at last, his piggy eyes screwed almost shut. 'But I keep hold of the shooter till we're outside and into your car.'

Taff hesitated, having in fact planned to snap on the cuffs the moment the gun was on the desk. In the event, it was Clough who decided it, nodding his head in agreement as he turned. 'You're on, then. Hide it in your coat and let's go.'

'What about documentary evidence?' Taff asked, accepting the compromise but far from happy with it. Guns always spooked the hell out of him, particularly in the hands of frightened villains. 'Anything incriminating on file? Discs or tapes, accounts, records of illicit payments, anything like that?' Then, at the man's startled headshake: 'It would greatly strengthen your side of the deal, reinforce your testimony.'

'No! God, you people really know how to push!'

'Forget it, then,' Clough cut in, gesturing towards the door. 'Let's get out of here.'

It was in Taff's mind to jump and disarm the man as he was covering the gun with his raincoat. However, thanks to Clough's haste to get out, the moment was lost. Once again, as they waited for the elevator, Taff braced in readiness for the chance to disarm him. But it arrived already half full with people so that he couldn't risk the chance of stray shots flying around—a risk which persisted as they left the lift and crossed reception to head out down the entrance steps to Cheapside.

'We're parked down Gutter Lane,' Clough remarked as they reached the pavement. He started to turn, only to pitch forward as Turnbull suddenly pistol-whipped him across the side of the head. The man swung round to loose off a couple of wild shots, one of which whacked Taff sideways, then he was sprinting for his life towards St Paul's.

In fact, had the fugitive realized it, he was virtually clear and away. Taff's pursuit was severely hampered by the flesh wound in his shoulder, waves of dizziness threatening to overwhelm him. That he managed to stagger on at all was due solely to that dogged Welsh obstinacy. Alan Turnbull, however, was hounded by a dread far more formidable than the crippled arm of the Law. No hiding-place indeed! So that he kept up his reckless pace around St Paul's and wildly along the full length of Newgate Street.

It was shortly after passing the tube station that, for no apparent reason other than blind panic, he switched course across the street, doing so almost under the wheels of a speeding BMW. The car's bonnet flung him into the air in a trajectory which, with the fugitive's own momentum, cartwheeled him sideways on to the parapet of Holborn Viaduct over which, as if in slow motion, his body toppled to crash fatally down into the traffic of Farringdon Street way below.

'It's a cancer, of course, of which BCCI and Lystons are typical. But the disease is of a type which the combination of greed, fear and the City's corporate system make it almost impossible to resist. I doubt, even if Alan Turnbull had lived to turn genuine supergrass, whether his testimony alone would have been anywhere near enough for the DPP to attempt a prosecution. Basically, the bigger the infected company, the more immune it is. Virtually, the only way they can ever go down is the way BCCI did—when those within become so diseased with greed that they loot their own Pandora's box.'

Kate had sat soaking up Taff's rhetoric with much the same relish that she was quaffing her wine—an excellent Rhône vintage sent to Taff as a get-well gift by her bastard editor.

'So anyway,' she remarked teasingly, 'you've finally decided to stay on in the force.'

'What?'

'Ralph Marsh and I had a bit of a chat around the time of your last annual review.'

'Cheek!'

'Not at all. He had identified somewhat of a career crisis.'

'The depth of my governor's perception constantly amazes me.'

'Anyway, you're now back on course, uh-huh?'

Taff sipped wine, taking his time before finally conceding her a rueful nod.

'All you really needed was to get away from PR and, like a vampire, get your fangs into a good solid murder.'

'Or two.' He grinned, baring those same fangs. 'Mind you, as usual I haven't done my career much good.'

'The bloody police! Why ever not?'

'All down the line everyone, me included, was saying the black pimp was guilty and deserved his life-sentence.' He grimaced at the irony. 'We were all of us right. And, but for that busybody PACE crusader, David Roberts, the poor bastard would still be serving his due sentence.'

'Taff, will you stop tearing at it! Give it a chance to scab over at least!'

The copper shrugged, raising his glass. 'Meanwhile,

Bella the FAME will come out of it with a thumping great
black-vote majority in the Brixton by-election.'

'For sure.'

'So there, you see.' He finished his wine and led his love
to bed. 'It's an ill wind . . .'